CORRUPTION
WITHIN

CORRUPTION WITHIN

Cesar Islas

To order additional copies of this book, contact:
Xlibris
844-714-8691
www.Xlibris.com
Orders@Xlibris.com
844246

CHAPTER 1

Making Arrangements with Stephanie

IT WAS THE LAST SATURDAY of September, about 7:30 a.m., to be exact. Michael was at his favorite place for breakfast, having three over medium eggs with some bacon and wheat toast with a cup of coffee. Right before he got his order, he had gotten a message from Casey. On her message, she stated how much she missed her dad and was curious when her dad was going to pick her up. As he read this, it broke his heart knowing how much she missed him. The feeling was mutual, but with him working undercover, it made it impossible for him to pick her up and give up his cover.

Michael had married Casey's mom, Stephanie, at an early age. Right after police academy, they dated for a few months, fell in love, and got married a few months later. The following year, Casey was born. Her birthday was on February 29, 2000. Michael had wanted a boy all along to take him fishing, hunting, and shooting and, as he grew up, to follow in his father's footsteps. He had wanted a boy so he could be an honorable police officer like his father. Just like Michael had followed in his father's footsteps. When Casey was born, Michael knew his dream would not be possible, and he would have to wait until their second-born child and wait and see if it would be a boy.

The marriage had lasted only about ten years. Stephanie was tired of spending too much time alone with Casey. Too much time away from her husband days, weeks, months without communication. She was tired of sleeping with that fear of waking up to that phone call letting her know her husband had passed away while on duty. At that point, Michael became realistic and knew women could be great at fishing and hunting, and they could also take good shots. Besides, with him being in the force for so long, he knew the station had great women doing an awesome job as well. Some were even way better at it than some men.

As he started to enjoy his breakfast, he replied to Casey at the same time. He did let her know he was working undercover at the time. He didn't know how much longer he would be on the case. Michael never did carry his personal phone when on a case. But ever since he got a divorce, he became the only person Casey had for emotional support whenever she would get into arguments with her mom. He had no other choice since he had determined he would be in her life as much as possible. She did say Halloween was just around the corner. She wanted to get an early start with her costume. She didn't want to wait till the end and not have lots of options on her costumes. He did let her know that as soon as he would get a break on the case, he would rush to her and spend some time with her.

As Michael was about to finish his breakfast, he got another message related to the case. He didn't get a chance to get a refill on his coffee as he wanted but instead got his gear and went on his way. As usual, he would meet with his captain at an undisclosed location to discuss issues about the case. Michael would give Captain Ross an update about what was going on and what was going to happen. Captain Ross would then determine what Michael's action would be until the following meeting.

Fortunately for Michael, Captain Ross had stated the undercover case had been going for almost nine months. They did have enough evidence to close the case and send their subject to jail for a while.

After hearing the news, Michael's eyes glared, and that brought him a smile. The captain noticed his face change and questioned Michael about it. He went ahead and told the Captain about how he had gotten a message from Casey asking for some father-daughter time. And as the case was being closed soon, that would hurry up the reunion between him and Casey. The Captain did know about Michael and his issues back home. How he was divorced and being one of Miami's greatest undercover officers. That really put him in a bind. He was aware that because of work, he had lost his wife. The captain didn't want him to lose his daughter as well.

Right before the meeting was over, the captain gave Michael the greatest news ever. "Michael, with the holidays just around the corner and you being undercover for nine months, I want you to start making some plans with Casey as soon as we close the case. I will not assign you to any more cases till next year. So with that being said, that will give you close to three to four months of time off."

That was like music to Michael's ears. He was anxious to call Casey and let her know the great news. He still had Stephanie to talk to. They did have a court order stating he was allowed to pick her up every Thursday for a few hours and every other weekend. As the holidays go, he would get even years, and she would get odd years. As per the summer, if he did give her a forty-five-day notice, he would be entitled to have Casey the whole summer, and then Stephanie would get the weekends. So with this year being 2015, Michael wouldn't have Casey this year. But with the great communication he and Stephanie had, he knew that wouldn't be a problem. Of course, a little heads-up and a few weeks' notice would help as well.

As soon as the meeting was over, the captain went his way, and Michael went his. On Michael's undercover case, he was a Canadian by the name of James Summers, wanting to establish a drug route from Miami all the way to Canada. Michael had bought a few kilos with his contact; that was a way to establish trust with them. A total of nine months had been enough to earn the trust of the drug cartel. So with that in place this week, Michael was going to set up the biggest drug deal Miami had ever seen. With the few kilos he had already bought off his contact, they had plenty of evidence to lock him up for good. But with the way the case went, they were going to have a chance to get a bigger fish. That's right, the drug supplier that was supplying Michael's contact. The whole force knew that would be a big bonus for the case. The undercover case was for a local dealer supplying and drugging kids in Miami. The force knew about it by word of mouth. But they didn't have the evidence to lock him up. Now it was a different story: one less dealer poisoning the life of our poor kids here in Miami.

Michael was on his way to meet up with his contact but was thinking way ahead. It had been a whole nine months away from Casey. He couldn't wait to hold her hug her and kiss her. He was trying to plan out a few things he had always wanted to do. Like going out deep-sea fishing. Maybe even some hunting. He loved bow hunting, and so did Casey. Since the last time they went out, Casey had gotten a lot better at it. Since crossbow hunting did run from September till November, that gave Michael lots more time to relax and do what he loved a lot.

Michael was coming from Coral Gabe's on Highway 1 toward Miami day dreaming away when he got a call. It was from his contact he wanted to set up a meeting have a quick lunch around noon time to set up the time and date of when the big deal was going to go down. Keeping in mind both were seafood lovers, they both agreed to meet at Sonia's down on eighth. By the time they hung up, it was past 10:00 a.m. That gave Michael two hours to spare. As he drove down to Miami, he remembered he still had to get everything set up with Stephanie as well. If she would say no and stick to her guns and say, "Every other weekend are yours," all his plans would be ruined for those three months with Casey. He grabbed his personal phone and dialed Stephanie. She must have been busy because she didn't answer his call. He went ahead and left her a voice mail and hung up the call. Before he put his phone down, it was already ringing. He was hoping it was Stephanie, but nope, it was his dad on the phone.

Like every day before noon, they would make an effort to stay in contact. If no one was available, they would leave each other a voice mail. Well, not this time. As the phone rang, Michael was thinking of what to tell him. He really wanted to call Stephanie back to get that resolved and find out if he was or wasn't gonna have Casey with him. As much as he wanted to talk to his dad, not this time. He let the call go to voice mail. He knew he would retrieve his message later and catch up with his dad at a later time. Once again, he tried reaching Stephanie back. This time she did answer. She said she had been in the shower at the time. They talked about their issues here and there and how each other's previous day had gone. Stephanie continued by stating how she had gone out on a great date. The place they had met at had been Joe's Stone Crab.

Michael being an officer and working all over Miami. He knew very well that place was well past Miami Beach over by Washington. He tried to change the subject at that point, because some jealousy had struck him. They had been divorced for a few years already, but it wasn't his choice. So yes, on Michael's behalf, there was still some love in his heart toward her. He automatically started letting her know about how quick the case was about to be closed and how much time he was going to have off. While telling her all this, not once did he ask if he could have Casey for the time being. He was thinking ahead. He knew if he asked her for that big favor of having Casey for this time off. He would be in big debt with her. At a later time, this would backfire on him and she could ask for another favor in return. If his reply would be no thank you at that point she would throw this favor in his face an at that point give him no option but to agree. So while he kept telling her about the whole three months off he would have an all the plans he had. Not once did he state Casey's name. So while he kept on and on, Stephanie questioned him about it.

"And how about my Casey? When are you gonna spend some time with her?"

Michael went ahead and played the good father's role and responded, "Well, I do have some activities to do with her every other Friday when I am supposed to pick her up."

As he made that comment, Stephanie's eyes watered and Michael noticed it in her voice. "You lost me already Michael because of lack of time at home. Don't do the same to her. Why don't you take her with you the whole time off? When I start missing her, bring her by, or we could have lunch or dinner and chat the night away."

Michael had felt so bad, especially after he had made her cry. He did get what he wanted, but he knew he had overdone it this time. Michael was about to reach his destination, and Stephanie had to get ready. Michael did let her know he would call her as soon as he would be available to pick Casey up. Stephanie's comments had gotten him as well, but he didn't want her to notice it. He had a lunch appointment as well, and he didn't want to arrive with his eyes all watery and red. He pulled over to cool off a bit. He got out of his car, leaned on the hood, and tilted his head up, staring at the clouds.

Michael wasn't much of a devoted Catholic as he would like. It wasn't by choice but cause of work as well. He closed his eyes and asked God for some help. He needed to clear his mind. With the case so close to being closed, he couldn't have his personal issues jeopardizing the whole case. By his experience, he knew something like this could cost him his life. Once his head was clear and he felt he was ready, he got back in his car and started to drive away to Sonia's to meet up with his contact.

CHAPTER 2

The Meeting

MICHAEL WAS THE FIRST TO arrive at Sonia's seafood restaurant. He approached the hostess and requested a table for two. As he sat down, he quickly ordered a Michelob Ultra draft beer and headed toward the restroom. He just wanted to wash his face so his contact would have no idea he had just been crying his lungs out. As he came back, the waiter was just arriving with his beer and offered him the menu. Michael had been there a few times already and decided to order appetizers. He asked the waiter to bring him some yucca stuffed with cheese and jalapeños to snack on while he waited. He was halfway through his snack followed by two beers.

As he was taking the last swig on his beer. He noticed Pedro's bodyguards walking in as usual. Every time they met, his two bodyguards would walk in, check out the place to make sure it's safe for Pedro, then give him the call to let him know whether it's safe for him to come in. Pedro was the contact Michael was working with. As far as Michael knew, he was working out of Texas Branching out in Florida, and Miami was his starting point. He had done so much damage to the local neighborhoods already, enough to get an undercover case on him. As he walked in, he had that great trust with Michael. He yelled out, "Que onda pinche guero donde esta esa mano amiga?" What's up white boy where's that friendly hand?

As Pedro sat down, he noticed Michael had some food already, and a beer as well. "Damn, James, looks like you're freaking hungry and couldn't wait for me."

"Damn, Pedro, you took a long-ass time. As soon as I got here, I was thirsty, and you know how great the food is. So I just got me an appetizer man, nothing big."

As they were chatting away, the waiter showed up again. James asked for another Michelob for him and a dressed Corona for Pedro. Pedro just smiled. "That's what I like about you, cabron [sucker]. You're getting to know me very well. At times, I don't know if that's good or bad, but only time will tell, don't you think."

James (Michael) was enjoying his appetizer. He didn't speak, just nodded his head as if agreeing with him. I would offer you some, Pedro, but I am on my last bite. Hope you don't mind."

"Don't worry, pinche guero [fuckin' white boy]. Eat away, my friend. Besides, once he comes with the menu, I am about to order already, don't worry."

When the waiter came back, he brought back two menus, dropped off the beers, and let them know to take their time. He would be back to take their orders in a bit. As they were both looking at their menu, Pedro looked at James (Michael).

"Hey, guero [white boy], how about we enjoy our meal, have some drinks, then after head over to my place and talk business."

James (Michael) took a chug of his beer and agreed they would both enjoy their meal a bit more if they did as he said. Once they were ready, they signaled the waiter, letting him know they were ready. Pedro got the Colas de Langosta al Ajillo (lobster tail in garlic sauce), and James ordered Camarones en salsa Verde (shrimp in green sauce). As soon as they both finished their meal, Pedro told James (Michael) it would be best if he left his car at the restaurant and they would both leave in his vehicle.

As they were both leaving, Pedro told him he had a few stops to make before they headed to his place. Hope he didn't mind. As they drove away, Pedro started telling James (Michael) about "your next shipment and the purpose of our meeting, my friend. We seem to have a little problem, but it ain't nothing we won't resolve."

"Problem?" James (Michael) replied. "How bad is it?"

"Well, you requested 40k for our next shipment, which we did have, but some locals down in Reynosa got a bit greedy, raided some of our houses, and took our stash. All we have is the 20k we have here in Miami for now. Don't worry, we are going to get you what you requested, but it's going to take us some time now. A bit longer than expected."

"How long is that wait?" James (Michael) replied.

"Well, I spoke to the big boss, and he was thinking it would be a great idea if you would fly down to meet up with him and spend some days down in Texas. He wants you to spend Dia de Los Muertos (Day of the Dead) with him."

"Is that a holiday? When is that celebrated?" James (Michael) asked. That's on November 2. Mexican Nationals take that time to spend it with the family members that have passed away. The big boss takes the time to honor those that have passed away, protecting his life and in honor of his brother that passed away in a gunfight a few years back."

James (Michael) knew that would change his whole plan. He was shooting at closing the case as soon as possible and starting to enjoy his vacation with Casey. "Damn, Pedro, that's really gonna suck, my friend. I got some holidays just around the corner as well. We celebrate Thanksgiving on the twelfth of next month now. If I miss that, I won't hear the end of it from my mom. Then I got Halloween at the end of the month. If I miss that, I will be sleeping on the couch for a whole month. Not good, my friend. Not good at all. Well, how about if we take half of the shipment, do we still get to meet the boss as we planned out?"

"No, my friend, the deal was the whole shipment. You get to meet the boss. If you agree to get half, I can give you that myself."

As he finished making that comment, the truck pulled over. Pedro got off and told James (Michael) to wait in the truck. The two bodyguards got off as usual and headed out. First, they gave Pedro the call, and he headed in their direction. That gave Michael time to think of what he was going to do. Yes, he loved his job. If he had to extend the case, he had no choice but to agree and wait. Besides, he wanted the big boss as well. He had loved the idea of killing two birds with one stone. He had the captain to speak to as well. He knew it wasn't gonna be his decision to take. He also had Casey to think of. She had been texting over and over about her Halloween costume as well.

Stephanie's comment came to his mind as well when she had said, "You lost me already. I don't want you losing her as well." As he was thinking all this, about thirty minutes had passed already, and Pedro and his bodyguards were nowhere to be seen. As James (Michael) looked around, he noticed they were in the most dangerous part of Miami. That place was known for having gunfights at random times of the day. Most of the time, it ended with deals gone wrong and a few bodies on the floor. As he remembered all this, he noticed two vehicles approached the location and four men carrying AK-47s walked into the same place Pedro and his men had walked in to. James (Michael) knew something had gone wrong. He needed to act quick if he wanted to come out of this one alive. James (Michael) noticed the bodyguard had left the keys in the ignition. He turned the truck on and took his gun out and walked toward the direction of the four men.

As soon as he got to the door, the gunfight started. They had bullets flying left and right. With the four men that went in after Pedro, that put Pedro and his bodyguards in a bind. Pedro and his men were surrounded by the bad guys. Pedro was aware of the situation 'cause Michael could hear him screaming, "Piss off, hijos de puta se les va llevar madres a todos!" (Sons of a bitch, everybody will pay for this!)

Michael slowly crept up on the four guys and took two out at a time. As soon as he had all four down, he signaled Pedro, letting him know the coast was clear. And he headed in Michael's direction with one of his bodyguards. The other had been seriously wounded, and it was impossible to get him out at the moment. The three of them left the place as fast as they could. Leaving the truck on made it a bit easier to leave the place. The gunmen were able to hit the truck, but nothing serious. The whole way to Pedro's place, he kept making phone calls left and right. He told every single person he spoke to, to meet him at his place as soon as possible. As soon as they got to his place, we quickly got off, and he rushed to give Michael a hug and a kiss on the forehead. "Gracias, puto." (Thank you, sucker.) "You saved my life. I owe you one. I won't forget this."

"Don't worry, that's what friends are for, ain't we. What the hell you want me around for if I can't defend you when your life depends on it?" James (Michael) replied.

"You got that right, cabron," Pedro replied. As they walked in to his place, Pedro pointed to the bar. There's the beer and liquor. Drink as you wish. I am going up to my room. If anybody arrives, invite them to some drinks. I will be down in a bit."

"Sure will, man. Don't worry, I got this," James (Michael) replied. He guessed Pedro was close to his bodyguards, or he held him after he got shot, because he was full of blood, and it wasn't his. He and the other bodyguard came out unharmed.

As Michael was having his drink, ten armed men showed up. Eight stayed outside, and two walked in. He shook both of their hands. One said, "You must be the Canadian, the man of the hour."

"Yes, sir, James Summers is the name. It's a pleasure to meet you."

"The pleasure is mine, James. I am Juan Gonzales, better known as El Pilas, here to assist you as you wish. The boss has spoken great about you. Especially today. Thanks to you, he is still with us today. If you ever have any issues with the northern part of Florida, I am the man to speak to."

As they were finishing with their introductions, another twelve armed men showed up. This time eleven stayed outside and one came in.

"James, this is El Yanko. He is the leader of our Cuban gang here in South Miami. They help us out with most of our dirty work."

"Hey, Yanko I am James. Nice to meet you."

"Well, Pilas, looks like we are about to get some payback. We got a whole army ready to attack."

"We will see about that, James. Once the boss comes out, he will give us instructions, and we will take it from there. Based on what the boss said, I wouldn't mind having you on my side, James," Pilas replied.

James just smiled. "We will see about that, my friend. Let's wait for your boss and see what he says."

As he finished making those comments, Pedro came down, still with a pissed-off face. He thanked Yanko and Pilas for showing up on such short notice.

"Have you guys met James? He will be our contact in Canada. Thanks to this man, I am alive today. Gentlemen, this is what we are going to do tonight. Pilas, you and Yanko, with all your men, will go back and give our friends a friendly surprise. I don't want you guys to leave the place till everybody in that place is wiped out . Make sure you all let them know who is in charge here." As Pedro was giving them the instructions, Michael interrupted him.

"Pedro, don't you think that's a bit too soon? They will be waiting for us to hit back tonight, they will double their men."

"No, my friend, that ain't the way our cartel works. We hit them tonight, and where it hurts. That will show them not to mess with us. And, my friend, thanks for saving my life, but you will not be included in this attack. We need you in Canada. We don't want anything to happen to you. Besides, this is our turf. You defend and protect Canada. We will do the same here in Miami. Pilas and Yanko, if you all feel you all need more men, take my guys as well. Just leave me two guys behind and head out."

As they were all leaving, Pedro walked with Michael to the bar, poured himself a drink, and made Michael one as well. "Let's toast to our new friendship and many more deals to come in the future. I will be getting in contact with the big boss. I will let him know about your reason not to meet up with him in November, and I will get in contact with you around Monday or so."

"Sounds like a plan. Hope we can work something out. Keep me posted," replied James. As he finished his drink, he walked out of Pedro's place and had one of his guards take him back to the restaurant to pick up his car. As soon as he got in his car, he called the captain to let him know of the change of plans. Another meeting was needed. The captain agreed, and he headed to their usual meeting spot. As he waited for the captain, he noticed it was a bit late already. He just messaged Casey with a "Good night, sweet dreams" message, hoping he wouldn't wake her up with his message but hoping she would see it in the morning when she would wake up. To his surprise, she wasn't asleep yet.

She replied about a minute after. "Same to you, Daddy. Good night."

As the Captain showed up Michael quickly briefed him about what had happed . He let him know the shooting down town was in connection to the case and told him it was going to get worse tonight. He made the captain aware their contact wasn't a small fish, as they had thought. He did have strong ties to the cartel and was controlling most of Miami all on his own. Then Michael proceeded to let him know there was a possibility they weren't going to be able to get the big boss unless he agreed to meet up with the boss in November, but that would only extend their case a bit longer.

The captain really didn't like the idea and replied, "No, Michael, we can't prolong this case any longer for two reasons. One, budget. I have the boss breathing down my neck already. We have all the information we need on our contact to open a case on him and send him to jail for good. Two, Casey. Michael, I don't want you to make her wait any longer. You know very well she needs you. I don't want to hold you back any longer if I don't have to, so don't worry about the big boss. If possible, just let them know we will be taking what they have, and case closed. We make our arrest, and you start your vacation, how about that."

"I love your way of thinking, boss, but you know how much I love my job. If you feel we have to extend it a bit longer, don't worry. I can explain it to Casey. Besides, she don't know when the case will be closed. She knows it's soon, but not soon enough."

"No, Michael," the captain replied. "It ain't gonna work like that. We got what we need. You head home, enjoy your weekend, and let's see what happens. But I am shooting for next weekend, Michael. What do you think about one more week on the case is enough."

"Sure, Captain, that should be enough. Have a great night. See you later."

As the captain drove away, Michael stayed behind. He hadn't showed how scared he had been, but deep inside, he was really scared. This last shooting was nothing compared to the ones before. He was used to being in charge when out in a shootout. This one was the opposite. They were in charge. He charged in and shot his way in. To his luck, it went his way unharmed. He was clearly understanding Stephanie's point of view now. When she stated she was afraid to get that call he wouldn't return from that case, he knew he didn't have anything to do for the next two days. He was supposed to meet Pedro no later than Monday. He drove away to his place, making a stop at the store to purchase some beer for the night. He knew it would hit the spot and make him feel a bit better.

CHAPTER 3

The Embarrassing Moment

ICHAEL GOT HOME AND DRANK the night away. He had overdone it because the following day, he didn't wake up till about 2:00 p.m. He picked up his phone and noticed some missed calls and text message from Casey. He replied to Casey and went to take a shower. His missed call was from his dad. He would call him back as soon as he came out of the shower. As he came out, he got ready and thought once again of all the great things he was planning to do with Casey. He knew he was missing a lot of gear for most of the extracurricular activities he was planning out. So his plan was to head out to Dick's Sporting Goods in downtown Miami. He knew he would find most or all the stuff they would need. Dick's was about a twenty-minute drive for him from the apartment. He had plenty of time to call his dad right back.

As he was talking with his dad, he got a call from an unknown number. The caller ID display only showed 01152, followed by more digits. He didn't know the number, so he didn't worry about it and kept talking with his dad. When he arrived at Dick's, he told his dad he had to go. As he walked in, he went straight to the fishing gear. They had so many fishing rods: some were small, others were about ten feet high. Michael knew they wouldn't be doing any pier fishing, so he wouldn't be needing the ten-feet fishing rods. The normal six feet would do for now. As he finished getting all the fishing gear he needed, he continued to the hunting gear. He had most of all he would probably need except for some arrows. But he loved looking at all the new gear they had anyways. He continued looking around. When he felt he was done with his shopping, he went straight to check out.

As he was waiting, he got a message from Casey: "Lumu dad a lot a bunch." He knew most of her abbreviations on her text messages, but he had gotten him on this one. He had no clue what "Lumu" meant. As he waited to pay for his items, he had his confused face on. As he was next to pay, he looked at the cashier and asked her, "Excuse me, ma'am, would you be able to help me out? I just got a text message from my daughter but don't have a clue what it means."

He gave her the phone, and she stared at the phone and read the message. As she read it, she looked up and grabbed her chin as if she was thinking about it. Then she continued and told Michael, "'Love You and Miss You a lot a bunch.' That's what your message means, sir." And she gave him his phone back and continued charging him for his items. He thanked her and offered to invite her to get a coffee at Starbucks.

The lady declined the invitation, stating she was there to help out without receiving anything in return.

Michael felt out of place. He had been out of the game for almost two years. He had or knew of no other way to approach her. He continued to pay and thanked her for her help. He had that embarrassed face as he walked away with his items. As he walked out, he texted Casey back with "Lumu right back at you baby." As he left Dick's, he felt like eating some steak, and with his time off for the weekend, he knew this was the perfect time to do so. With him working undercover, he couldn't just call his friends and have a cookout with them. So he had to settle with a solo cookout for now. He stopped by the meat market and bought himself a forty-dollar barbecue package they had, followed by another 18-pack. He knew he had a long weekend to go.

As he paid with cash, he got another call from the same number as before. He still didn't have a clue who it was and didn't bother to answer the call. He let it go to voice mail again and left the meat market. He headed back to his place turned on the pit and opened another beer while he got the meat cut and seasoned. With all he had in mind, those beers were kicking in super good. Once again, he drank the night away.

It was a way of releasing all his stress. Once again, he drank all night and woke up super late the next day. He woke up super hungry. He knew his favorite place for breakfast would just hit the spot. He got up, got ready, and headed out for breakfast. He had been there so many times some of the waiters knew him by name already. Good morning, sir, will you be having the usual followed by a cup of coffee?

"Yes, please," Michael replied and headed out to his usual table. As he waited for his food, he remembered the embarrassing moment he had yesterday at Dick's. He thought of ways to make up for that moment. He hadn't been in the game that long. His best option was to order some flowers for her. He got on his phone and googled a nearby flower shop and made the call. When they answered, he requested for some nice colorful flowers. The lady suggested some roses. Michael felt roses were too much. The arrangement was more of a thank you, not an "I love you" message. He just went ahead and asked for an arrangement of colorful carnations.

"On your card what message would you like?"

Michael thought about it and replied, "'Thank you for your help. It meant a lot.' Signed, 'Starbucks guy.' As he continued to pay, he realized he was missing one credit card. He automatically got his backup one and paid for the flower arrangement. As he hung up, he tried to backtrack on his steps and figured out where he could have left his card. He knew that at the meat market, he had paid with cash. The other place he thought about was Dick's. He googled the number and requested to speak to customer service manager. He told him his situation, and the manager put him on hold as she went out to see if anybody had turned in a forgotten credit card. When she came back on the phone, she went ahead and told him he had left it behind; the credit card was in their possession.

Michael informed her he would be in to pick it up as soon as he had a chance. It really wasn't his credit card. It belonged to James Summers. It was the one he had been using while undercover. If he lost it, he wouldn't hear the end of it from his captain. By the time he was done ordering the flowers, his order was already at this table. He requested the waiter for today's newspaper as well. As he enjoyed his breakfast, he was reading the front-page Maine news. "Drug Deal Gone Wrong." The newspaper stated that there was a total of fifteen dead and gunshots all over the place. No survivors. They mentioned possible ties to local dealers in the area. They also mentioned local gangs wanting to make a name for themselves.

What they couldn't understand were the two old English letters painted on the wall. As per the newspaper, they left the SA initials in old English. He put the newspaper away and continued enjoying his breakfast. He called the captain and requested a meeting. The captain agreed to meet up in about an hour. When the captain arrived, Michael was already there. Michael explained to the captain the purpose of their meeting was to get more information about the shooting reported in the newspaper. Michael questioned the captain about the two initials left behind as well. The captain informed Michael that next to the initials, they left a message in Spanish that read, "The boss has arrived."

They still couldn't put two and two together as far as where or what "SA" means . "We don't have any local gangs with those initials here in town. Not unless it's a new gang coming in to town, that's my only explanation."

As they were both discussing the whole news, Michael got another call from the same number again. He quickly gave the number to the captain and asked him to search it up and try to get some information on it so he could get an idea of who it was or what they wanted. Michael then proceeded to inform the captain that he had made some purchases with the case credit card that had nothing to do with the case. Michael explained he didn't want to waste time purchasing items he would need when the time came. He thought it would be easy to use the case credit card and do the paperwork on how much he owed when the case was closed.

The captain just took notes. "If the office doesn't make a big deal over the purchases, don't worry. I won't say a thing, Michael." Then the captain informed him he would get back with him as soon as he had more information on the number he had just given him. The captain went on his way, and Michael remembered he still had to pick up the credit card. He got in his vehicle and headed on to pick it up.

He remembered about the flowers and followed to call the flower shop. The flower shop informed Michael the flowers had been delivered about thirty minutes ago.

A soon as he got to Dick's, they asked him for some identification to confirm the credit card was indeed his. As he picked it up, he saw the sticky pad note on in.

> Awww, that was sweet Mr. Starbucks. I really loved the flowers and my answer is yes. I sure would love to have that coffee with you. Call me when ever you get a chance

Michael had loved the idea of calling her, but he still had some errands to run and was still working the case. He didn't want to get her involved. And what if the case went south? He would put her in danger. So that first call sure was gonna wait. For how long? Well, till the case would be closed for now.

CHAPTER 4

The Unexpected Trip

ICHAEL REFUSED TO CALL SALLY. For now, he continued to do his errands for the day. It was getting late. Michael did a quick stop at the liquor store once again, but this time he got a bottle of Cazadores Reposado. Once he purchased the bottle, he drove back to his place and drank the night away. The following morning, he woke up with a super bad headache, took some pills, and took a quick shower. As he came out of the shower, he noticed two missed calls from the same strange number, one from Pedro, and another from his dad. He had a message from Casey telling him how much she missed him and was counting the days till he picked her up.

He replied to Casey first. "I Lumu too, baby. Daddy will be picking you up soon, I promise." Then he proceeded to read Pedro's message: "Where are you, man, answer your phone." Once he was dressed, he followed to call Pedro.

"What's up, man? What's going on, what's the urgency?"

"Man, the boss has been calling you and calling you for days now. Your time has arrived. He wants to meet you, James."

"My time has arrived, what you mean meet me? Where, is he in town?"

"No, James, the Boss is back home in Texas. I told him your issue about the holidays and not being able to meet up with him in November. So he wants me to fly you down to Texas today. Don't overdo it with your packing. Just bring the essentials. I will forward you my address, meet you there in an hour."

"Wait, Pedro, I have stuff to do. I can't just get up and leave."

"James, the Boss don't like to wait, and he don't take no as an answer. He don't take people to his place that often. You should be flattered. He normally meets people at undisclosed location, never at his place. With you, he strictly instructed me to take you to his place. Once you meet him, James, we will control all of North America. The boss will have control of Mexico and South America. I will have control of the USA, and you, my friend, of course, you got Canada. So get your shit together quick and let me send you my address."

Michael, at that point, had no choice but to agree to the trip. He had no other option as the captain had agreed the case would be closed this coming Saturday. He still was six days away. "Sure will, Pedro. Send me the address. See you there in an hour." Michael just bagged the essentials as Pedro had requested. Then he got in his car and drove down to Miami. On his way down, he called the captain to let him know of the changes in the case. The captain must have been busy because he didn't answer his call. Michael had no choice but to leave him a brief voice message for now.

Michael wanted to be a bit more careful with this trip. He didn't want to expose himself at this point in the case. So he decided to leave his phone behind. He sent Casey a brief message letting her know he would be out of town and wouldn't be able to reply to her messages. Casey must have been at school at the time he sent the message because she didn't reply as quickly as she normally would. When he arrived at Pedro's place, he left his phone and just took his wallet he carried with James Summers's information.

When he arrived, he followed to admire the home. It was almost a replica of Tony Montana's mansion in the movie *Scarface*. With almost the same number of bodyguards, it felt to Michael as though he was about to visit the president. That's how big and powerful Pedro was getting here in Miami. The captain was right. They needed to close this case a soon as possible.

As he walked in to the home, he was searched by the bodyguards. Pedro followed to call them off. "No need to do so, Chaco. I owe my life to that man. He has all my trust."

"Come in, James. Welcome to my humble home, amigo [friend]).

"Damn, Pedro, you got one hell of a mansion here. My home in Canada ain't as big as this one I am jealous with you, man."

"Don't be, my friend. With the business we are about to do, will give you enough money to buy close to one hundred homes like this one."

"I have known you for almost nine months. I hadn't seen this home. Did you just purchase it?" Michael was trying to gather more information on Pedro just in case. You never know if it was needed when it came to his time in court.

"You got that right," replied Pedro. "I just got it about three months ago. I hardly bring people here. This is my vacation home. The others you have seen are the homes where I conduct my deals."

"I see," replied James.

"Hey, about that shootout, what happened after all? I read in the newspapers you guys left no survivors. The press and cops are blaming some new gang in town due to some initials and some Spanish message left behind."

Pedro just smiled and questioned him about it. "How do you know about the message? I have been reading the newspapers, and on the report, it didn't say a thing about the message."

James just returned his smile back. "Just 'cause I am from Canada don't mean I have powerful people in the force."

Pedro felt a relief with his reply. "I am glad you mentioned that. Hope it ain't the same people we have . We need more people on the inside to help us out in the long run."

Pedro's comment got James thinking he had been on the force long enough. He knew almost everybody. Not one looked like they would sell out, but guess he was wrong. He didn't think much of it anymore. Pedro got his bag and tapped James.

"Let's go, it's time. We can't keep the boss waiting." They drove away to the airport, did the whole checkout, and headed toward a small private plane.

"We are flying in this Pedro?" James asked.

"Of course, man. The boss sent his private little toy to pick us up."

As they flew away, Pedro took a quick nap, and James sat on the window side. He glared out the window, thinking of Casey and their vacation and all the plans he had with her as well. He was also thinking of Sally. He wanted to call her so bad, get the nervous urge out of him once and for all. He knew once he got that first meet-and-greet date out of the way, he would feel way much comfortable with her. As they arrived in McAllen, Texas, a black SUV was waiting for them. They both got their bags and got in the vehicle. On their way to the border, Pedro acted as his personal tour guide all the way to Mexico.

"Look, James, this my home, El Valle. I started here, my friend. The Boss first left me here in charge all alone . It was a bitch at the beginning competing with Junior for the territory till the Boss told him I had earned it and he would have to wait."

"Junior?" James asked. Have I met him?"

"No, man, he stayed behind in Miami. I left him in charge while I came down to meet up with the Boss. You probably won't meet him till a later time. Maybe when we close the deal, he might be there—that's if he don't come home, but we will see." As Pedro was explaining to James, James realized they were reaching a border.

"Pedro, where are we going? That looks like a checkpoint."

"It is, my friend. Don't worry," Pedro replied. "Remember, I told you the boss wanted me to take you to his place, not his business homes here in the Valley. And that home is in Reynosa, my friend. Don't worry, we control Reynosa as well. We got this. If we get stopped, don't worry. I will do all the talking."

"OK," replied James. He had no other choice. He was already in the vehicle; he had no way out. They crossed the border with no problems at all. Once they got in to Reynosa, Tamaulipas, they had a checkpoint up ahead. The driver informed Pedro of the situation.

"Do we go back and go around, boss? We don't have the guns or men to take them on."

"No," Pedro replied. "We ain't doing nothing wrong other than driving through town. Go ahead."

When they reached the checkpoint, an officer approached the vehicle. "Buenas tardes, soy el official Romero. Hola, Pedro, k ávido cabron me encanta cuando ustedes de pendejos me asen el trabajo más facil." (Good afternoon, I am Officer Romero. Pedro, how are you doing, sucker? I love it when you dumbasses make my job way much easier.)

"Vajale de huevos cabron que no se te olvide de quien eres llerno que si no fuera por el ya no estuvieras aquí para contarla," Pedro replied. (Lower your tone of voice, sucker. Don't forget who your father-in-law is. Otherwise, you wouldn't be alive to tell about it.)

The officer just smiled and stated, "Voy a ser un chequeo de rutina que si allo tan solo una arma oh drogas en la camioneta se les va cargar el payaso a todos." (I will continue to do my routine checkup. If I find a gun or drugs in the vehicle, I will take all of you guys to jail.)

The officer continued to do his routine checkup on the vehicle and had them all get off to do so. James could tell this guy wasn't on Pedro's payroll because he sure was giving him a hell of a hard time. He didn't find anything wrong and let us go, but not before he made another comment. "Se fueron de rallas pinches perros pero tarde oh temprano se les va cargar la chingada a ti y a todo su pinche cartel, cabron." (You got lucky, you filthy dog. But sooner than later, I will take down you and your whole cartel.)

As they were leaving, Pedro told James off from head to toe all the way to the location. James interrupted him by asking, "I thought this was your town and had everything is under control, Pedro?"

"That motherfucker will pay for that one day, James. His father-in-law is the governor of Tamaulipas. He is in our payroll. He lets us work without any issues as long as we don't touch his family. And that sucker just happens to be one of them. One day, man, one day, I promise they will find his body in one of the drain ditches we have here in Reynosa, but without a head. I promise you that."

When they arrived at the location, they went through three rings of security before they reached the home. As they got off, they got received by a gentleman dressed in a fancy red silk robe and wearing slippers.

"James, would you prefer our conversation in Spanish or English?"

"English please," James replied.

"I am Checo. Welcome to my humble home. Pedro has been talking so many good things about you that I extended the courtesy of inviting you to my humble home."

"The pleasure is mine, Checo."

"Come in, I have what we call a pachanga set up for us tonight. Hope you like cabrito, that's going to be our main dish."

As he walked in to the home, James noticed the same old English letters that Pedro's crew had left behind at the shootout the other night on the back of his robe. As they walked in, Checo ordered the kitchen ladies to serve the meal. His visitors had arrived and he was supper hungry already. He directed his guests to the dinner table, where they started talking about business.

"Well, James, the purpose of this visit was to get to know the man Pedro has been talking about for so long. He has been doing business with you for a while already. And as far as I know, I have a question for you. For the last nine months, you have been purchasing about four kilos a month from us. Now you have asked for forty kilos. That's a big difference."

"Glad you asked, Checo. I don't know if Pedro has told you already. Canada cartel is controlled by several of us, not just me. At the beginning, we were supplying parts of Canada and the rest was controlled by the other cartel. Well, it happens they have gotten a taste of our shipments and they want to join forces with us. The deal was we would supply the drug and have the majority of the vote when it came to changes or new rules of territory issues. They agreed, and here I am," James stated.

"Sounds like a legit answer, I should say," replied Checo. I don't know if Pedro has given you a price per kilo already, but this is my offer. Let me know if you take it or leave it. We won't be giving you our kilos at the same price as we sell them in Florida. We will be giving you our Texas price. That should save you a few thousands every time we make a deal. Now on top of that, we will be supplying you with our best shit we got. We won't even make a cut in it. That should make the merchandise a whole lot better than what you have been getting."

"What's the catch to all this?" James asked.

Checo just smiled and replied, "You're a very smart man, James. Well, the catch is this: not only will I be your main supplier, but I want to be the man you come to in times of trouble. Before you make a decision, you will consult it with me first, then your contacts in Canada. So what do you think, do we have a deal?"

James knew Checo was full of shit. No cartel would accept his deal in the real world. But he wasn't in a position to set his standards. This whole undercover case was set up to catch Pedro. Catching Checo was just gonna be a *bonus*. James gave him a smile, got up from his seat, and extended his hand. Sounds like we will be joining forces, Checo. You have yourself a deal. Besides business,it's all about money and power, ain't it."

They both shook hands, and Pedro followed with a toast. "This toast is for the most powerful man in all Latin America." They all took a chug of their beer and celebrated with Pedro. Right after the toast, the food arrived, and they all followed to be seated at the dinner table. James had never had cabrito before. It looked good, but looks could be deceiving. They all ate, and it was as good as it looked. The charro beans with the salsa was damn the best meal James had had in a while.

As they were all enjoying their meal, James noticed the main picture in the center part of the room. It was Checo with two boys. They didn't look past twelve. Checo noticed James looking at his picture on the wall and followed to comment. "Those will be the rulers of all this one day. They ain't that small anymore. Junior is twenty-four. Now he is up in Miami helping Pedro with his new turf. Which he has been doing great up to now, expanding this empire for them. Ramiro, the smaller of them two is down in Central America. He is in charge of our shipments. He comes home every so often.

"I see. Lovely family," James replied. As they all finished their meal, Checo directed everybody to the patio. "Well, James, I hope you like this second part of our get-together."

He made a hand signal, and the guards brought about ten girls over. At that point, a live group started playing Spanish music. They started playing some nice songs because right after it started, Checo pulled out his gun and unloaded the gun straight in the air.

"That's my corrido, James. El Jefe De Jefes."

He brought James two girls and stated, "hope you have a great time."

James wasn't sure he wanted to go ahead with it. The whole time he was in Mexico, he still had Sally in his mind. He continued to drink, and the girls took him out to the dance floor a few times. He didn't have a clue what he was doing, but he was having a great time. He didn't have a clue how long they were out drinking. What he did know was he was waking up to two beautiful women in his bed. He was in shock, didn't have a clue if he had gone through with it and had done a great job or if he had fallen asleep and crashed the whole bed party.

As he was thinking of all this, one of the two girls woke up and stated, "Damn, papi, can we have a round 2?"

That comment made him feel so good he didn't remember a thing, but he knew he had done a great job based on what she was asking for.

CHAPTER 5

Coming Back Home

T WAS TUESDAY MORNING. PEDRO and James had finished having breakfast with the boss. You could see with their face reaction they both weren't feeling that great, but they both still managed to smile and comment to every question or comment the boss would ask. The boss wanted them to stay a few more days. He was really having a great time with them both. James had really earned the trust the boss was needing from him.

Pedro and James both agreed they would fly out at noon to arrive in Miami no later than 5:00 p.m. The boss gave him his number to his satellite phone. If you ever need anything, this is the number you need to dial to get in contact with me. They both gathered the few stuff they took on their trip down to Mexico both in one of the trucks, and the boss ordered his gunmen to take them to the airport. It was five thirty in Miami by the time they landed. James informed Pedro he would head out to Canada, get with his colleagues, and he would call him back to set up delivery options. He did tell him not to worry about the full load. They wouldn't mind getting half then a few days or weeks later get the rest.

Pedro didn't mind. He did state, "If possible, get the money no later than Saturday for the full load."

James agreed, and both went their way. He was anxious to text Casey to see how her day had gone. He also needed to get in contact with the captain to give him the update of what went on in Mexico. The case was supposed to close out this coming Saturday, but Michael had new information there was possibility the captain would change his mind. But he would find out as soon as they spoke. He also needed to text or call Sally. He was curious to know how that would be. He did remember they had a Starbucks date pending. He started his drive back to Hollywood with a big smile from ear to ear. He didn't know if it was because of the drinks, the music, or the cabrito he had for dinner. It sure wasn't because of the two girls he had when he woke up the following day because he didn't remember a thing of what went on in the bedroom.

As soon as he arrived at his place, he quickly went to his hidden compartment, were he had hidden all his personal items. He quickly got his phone and turned it on. He noticed his phone was swamped with incoming voice mails, missed calls, and texts. One by one, he replied to all the text messages he had gotten. He just took a little more time on Casey's text. He really wanted to let her know how much he missed her. He looked for the note Sally had left behind with the card to get her number and send her a quick text. He was gonna have to really sit down and think about what he was gonna tell her. She knew him as James Summers, or the Starbucks guy, which he liked better. As he sent her his first message, he wanted to wait and see how it would turn out. Besides, he was going to have his first coffee date with her. Now the case wasn't closed yet. He didn't want to get her involved in his life yet. He might run the risk of endangering her life if the whole case went south on him.

While he was thinking all this, he got a reply from Sally that said, "Well hello stranger. How have you been?" With that reply, he knew she wasn't bothered that he hadn't texted her or called her. As soon as he replied, he called the captain to let him know he was back in town. The captain's call went straight to voice mail. He had no other option but to leave him a voice mail and to let him know he would need a meeting a.s.a.p.

He called his dad right after and had a long chat with him. He said his goodbye about thirty minutes later.

As soon as he hung up, he had another text from Sally and Casey. Sally's message asked how true was he when he asked her out for a coffee date. Michael replied that he was really looking forward to meeting up, but at the moment, he was out of town. He looked at Casey's message: she was asking again, when was the going to pick her up? She was really anxious to spend time with him already. She also reminded him about her costume shopping. He told her the feeling was mutual; he would have an answer for her no later than today. He knew as soon as he spoke to the captain, he would have an answer.

He tried calling the captain again, and this time he did answer his phone. "Captain, I am back. We need to meet up. How about we do so in an hour?"

"See you there," the captain replied.

Before he went in to the restroom to take a shower, he got another reply from Sally. She stated how she understood the situation but was looking forward to meeting up as well. She told him break was over. If he texted back and she didn't reply, reason was she was working already. He didn't bother to reply, took his shower, and headed out to meet up with the captain.

As soon as the captain saw Michael, he gave him a big hug. You had me nervous, boy. You had me praying and lighting candles all night, praying to God you came back alive."

"Come on, boss. Everything turned out OK. I got some great news. I met the big boss. I finally got his trust. It's up to you if you still want to kill two birds with one stone."

"No, Michael, just take it as a fun getaway for you. I have my boss breathing down my neck already, Michael. Let's just close the case as we had agreed so you can enjoy your time off."

"I was just thinking the same, boss. You don't have an idea how many times Casey texted me, asking me over and over when was I going to pick her up."

The captain just smiled and replied, "I bet, Michael. It has been nine long months. So Saturday it will be. I am supposed to meet up with him and deliver the money. They want 800k for the amount we asked for."

"Glad you brought that up, Michael. I was only able to get 400k. They won't release any more money for undercover operations."

"We might have overdone it on the size of load we asked for."

''Well, Michael, let's hope all goes great. Do you want to be part of the operation on Saturday?"

"Not if I don't have to, boss. I would really love to start my vacation as of right now, if possible."

"You have earned it, Michael. Enjoy your time off, say hi to Casey and Stephanie for me."

CHAPTER 6

Michael's First Date

MICHAEL HAD SPENT ALMOST TWO hours with the captain. As he was driving into town, he got a message from Sally. "Just got out of work here at our meeting point just missing my date. Nowhere to be around lol."

As he was reading the message, he thought about stopping by. But then he thought about the conversation. What would he talk about? He really thought about the worst situation he had in his life and still managed to come out alive. This would only be a coffee date. He knew he would be OK. Without thinking about it twice, he turned around and headed to Starbucks.

He replied, "Order me a Frappe no whip cream be there in 5."

He called Stephanie right after. The phone rang an rang, but no answer. He left her a voice mail. "Need to speak with you asap call me back please."

As soon as he arrived at Starbucks, he remembered to text Casey. "Baby I have great news. Daddy will finish his paper work today. As soon as you get home, get your stuff ready will stop by and pick you up tonight no later than 10 pm Lumu a lot a bunch."

As soon as he sent the message, he got the courage to go off and meet Sally. But this time, she wouldn't be behind a cash register. As soon as he walked in, Sally noticed him walk in. She had her eyes wide open like in shock.

"You were being honest about being here in five. I didn't order anything for you. Besides, ain't you supposed to be out of town? That ain't the correct way to get to know someone. Starting with lies, James. If that's your real name."

She got her coffee and rushed out of Starbucks. He ran out right behind her. By the time he got in his car, a few more had driven in. He couldn't get out as quickly as he wanted. He did see the direction she took but wasn't quick enough. To his luck, all the lights turned red on him. He had no option but to turn the sirens on. Sally had about two blocks on him if she didn't take any turns and drove straight, and he assume he would catch up with her in no time. The traffic was bad. Michael was running the risk he wasn't going to be able to catch up with her.

There was a cop hiding behind Subway on Bob Hope Drive. Sally must have been speeding because he also turned his sirens on and pulled her over. He approached Sally to inform her of the traffic violations she had committed and said he would have to give her a citation for it.

As the officer walked back to his car to fill out the ticket, Sally sent Michael a text. "Thanks to you, I just got pulled over."

As Michael read this, he turned his radio on to hear the report information and location of the citation. As soon as the dispatcher came back with Sally's information over the radio, Michael rushed to the location. He signaled the officer and told him the situation. The officer happened to be one of Michael's old friends and agreed to make the citation a written warning. Michael asked for the warning citation and informed the officer he would give it to her.

As the citation officer drove away, Michael approached the car. Sally was about to give her verbal excuse and see if she could talk her way out of the ticket when she saw James approach her window.

"Good evening, ma'am, I am Officer Michael Brown with the Miami Police Department. I would like to explain that not only did I have an embarrassing moment, but I also just had a misunderstanding with a beautiful woman at Starbucks a few minutes ago. I was wondering if that beautiful woman would accept a dinner invitation at Omar's Seafood."

Sally was still in shock over what was going on. One moment she had her hopes up that James could be the one. Then she was rushing out of Starbucks thinking he was like most men, that all they do is lie, get what they want, and never hear from them. Now she had James, whose real name now was Michael, who is an officer. All this time, Sally still hadn't said a word back. She was still in shock.

Michael tapped the car with his keys, making a bit of a loud noise, hoping Sally would snap out of it. When she did, she apologized to Michael a few times and agreed to have dinner. She did state she couldn't stay out late on a school night. Michael agreed. He knew he couldn't either. He had Casey to pick up around ten o'clock that night.

As soon as they arrived, the hostess sat them down and took their drink orders. Michael once again introduced himself as Michael Brown. He did give her a slight explanation. He did let her know that because of work, he couldn't give her all the information as he liked. Sally, at this point, knew and acknowledged he had a point. While they both had dinner, they both talked about themselves and shared information about each other as though they've known each other for years. That was the feeling Michael wanted to have when he met her. And so did Sally. It was like they were both meant for each other. To make the conversation longer and spend more time chatting the night away, both ordered some dessert. It was like both didn't want to leave yet. They both felt as though they still had lots of information about each other to share.

As they both chatted away, Michael got a call from Stephanie. She had heard his voice mail and was returning his call. Michael was really enjoying his conversation with Sally, so he sent the call to voice mail. A few minutes later, she called back. Sally noticed a new call from the same number. She told Michael, "Don't mind me. If you have to take the call, go ahead. I don't mind."

Michael refused the call again and sent Stephanie an automatic text. "I am in a meeting. Will call you back." Stephanie replied with an "OK." And Sally and Michael both continued to chat away. The topic of being single and divorced came about, and Sally wanted to know his reason.

Michael wasn't sure he was ready for that. It wasn't nothing bad. It wasn't like he had cheated on her. He just wasn't sure she would like the whole idea of being alone for long periods of time. He knew he was gonna have to let her know sooner or later but was trying to avoid the topic for now. He turned the question around and asked her for her side of the story. What was her situation or reason of her being alone? Michael liked the fact she was a talker. All he would do was say yes or just nod his head and agree with her. He had been out of the dating scene for a while so her doing the talking was helping out a lot. He also had the pressure of saying the goodbye. Would he close it with a hug and no kiss, or would he go for the kiss in the cheek? Or would she want one in the lips? He didn't want to look desperate or disrespect her as well. He wanted to be like a true gentleman.

Without knowing it, time had flown right before their eyes. It was past 9:00 p.m. already. She had to head home, and Michael had to pick up Casey. He knew he had gotten safe this time. There was no time left for him to let her know of his situation. That was exactly what he wanted. He wasn't ready to give her all the information yet. He knew he had to, but just not now. He asked for the check and followed to pay and walked her out to her car. They both said goodbye several times, but neither one would move. Sally wouldn't get in her car and drive away. And Michael wouldn't leave and get in his car either. They both gave each other a very strong hug, as though they didn't want to let go.

Michael knew what butterflies in the stomach felt like. The problem was he hadn't felt them in a very long time. Sally must have felt something similar because they let go a few times and gave each other the eye contact, but neither one would take the initiative of taking the first kiss and would hug each other again. Not until Michael's phone vibrated. He had realized it must have been ten o'clock, or a bit past ten. He remembered he had told Casey he would pick her up around that time. He knew if he was gonna give her a kiss, now was the moment.

CHAPTER 7

Vacation time

THE DAY HAD ARRIVED. MICHAEL was anxious to spend time with Casey. The captain had stated he would take care of the operation to arrest Pedro on Saturday. So with that being said, Michael took his word and started his vacation. His first date with Sally had started a bit badly, but over all, it had turned out great. As he drove off from his dinner date, he called Stephanie. After the third ring, Casey answered the phone.

"Mom's taking a shower, Dad. When are you gonna pick me up? I miss you so, so much, you don't have an idea."

"I miss you too, baby. Are your bags packed already as I asked you earlier?"

"Yes, Dad, I got those ready as soon as I got your message. Just one question, Dad. How long am I staying with you, because I only packed clothes for two weeks," asked Casey.

"Two weeks, that should be OK, baby. We still have to do some shopping. I have some vacations planned out for us. When we head home, we can talk about it. Have your mom call me as soon as she gets out from her shower. For now, let her know I am on my way, baby. See you in thirty minutes or so," stated Michael. As he drove down Highway 1, he turned his radio on and tuned in to his favorite country station. Halfway to Homestead, Stephanie called him back. He lowered the radio and followed to answer her call.

"Michael, did you call? What happened?" asked Stephanie.

"Yes, I did just want to let you know I am off the case and I am on my way to pick up Casey. Be there in a bit," said Michael.

"I am so glad to hear that, Michael. I had an idea you were on your way already 'cause this one is hopping along all over the house. The only question I have is, how long are you going to keep her? When does your next undercover case start?" asked Stephanie.

"Well, I was thinking of keeping her till next year if possible. The captain put me on leave of absence, or something like that, and won't put me on a case till sometime next year, so that should give me about three months off to spend with Casey, if you don't mind," said Michael.

As he had made his comment to Stephanie, he got a text message from Sally. He decided to ignore it for now since he was on a call at the time. Stephanie didn't make a comment and stayed silent for a while. Michael had to call her out for her to respond.

"Are you still there, Stephanie? Hello."

"Yes, Michael, I am still here. It's just that three months away from her is going to be a lot of time for me. I don't know if I will be able to survive that long. If I miss her, would I be able to pick her up at least for the weekend, Michael?

"Sure, why not just give me a heads-up? I do have some road trips planned out for us. I don't want you to make some plans and for us to be away and it won't happen."

"Yeah, I know what you mean. I will keep that in mind," said Stephanie. They chatted away without realizing Michael had arrived at their home to pick Casey up.

"Stephanie, I am already outside. Can you let Casey know so we can head back home. I got a long drive back. You know it's about two hours back to West Palm Beach."

"Yes, I will let her know the door is open if you want to come in," said Stephanie.

"No, it's OK, I am going to stay behind and make some room in the car for Casey's luggage. Knowing her, she is bringing enough gear for a whole army."

Stephanie just laughed and confirmed his comment. "Yes,she is, Michael, just wait and see."

As Michael stayed behind to make room for Casey's stuff, as he had said he would, he also took the time to read and reply to Sally's text message. He got his phone and read her message. "Thank you for that great dinner. I had an awesome time with you. It seems we still have a lot to talk about. Hope to hear from you soon. Good night."

"Hey there, glad you enjoyed it. Can't wait to meet up with you again and continue where we left off. Good night, chat with you tomorrow." As he finished replying to Sally's message, he noticed Casey walking out of the house.

"Dad, Dad, I need your help. I got too many bags to carry. Help me please . . ."

Michael just smiled as he had assumed Casey had brought a total of three suitcases all full of clothes, her curling iron, and blow dryer. You name it, she had it packed and ready to go. Casey gave her mom a big hug and a kiss and said goodbye. Casey had never been away from Stephanie for that long. Stephanie knew those were going to be the longest three months of her life.

Michael approached Stephanie, noticed her watery eyes, and commented, "Don't worry, she will be fine. She will be one phone call away. Don't forget to call ahead of time whenever you want to pick her up. Till then, enjoy your free time."

Casey got in the car, and so did Michael, and they started their long two hours' drive to West Palm Beach. On their way home, Michael started telling Casey of all the plans he had for her.

"So, baby, how do you feel about going out hunting, fishing, and camping?"

"Dad, it all sounds good, but don't forget about school. I still have school I need to attend, did you forget about that?"

Michael had totally forgotten about that. All his vacations were made without thinking. Casey still had school. He looked at Casey and told her honestly, "Baby, I had totally forgotten about school. Looks like we might have to change our plans a bit. Hope you don't mind."

"Not at all, Dad. What matters is that we will be together. We can still plan out trips, but on the weekends only. If you had planned out trips, that would take a week or so. We can cut them out and enjoy them for two days and be back on Monday for school."

"Yeah, we could do that, baby. Sounds like we can still have a great time after all."

"Dad, can I ask you something?"

"Sure, baby, what's up? Where are we gonna stay this whole time I am gonna be with you?"

"At home, baby. Where else did you wanna stay?"

"Well, Dad, the reason I was asking was because I have school, and it will be kind of hard for both of us to drive back and forth Monday to Friday. You do realize it's more than an hour's drive to get home from Mom's house."

"Honestly, baby, I hadn't thought about that either. Once again, I didn't remember about school when I made my plans. All I was thinking was just spending time with you, baby. Tell you what, why don't you take a day off tomorrow from school while we preplan our whole time together."

"Dad, a day off from school sounds good to me." She removed her seat belt and gave him a hug and a big kiss. I really missed you a lot, Dad. We hadn't spent that much time together in a while."

"I missed you too, baby. But I promise after this vacation, it's all going to change. I promise it will."

"Really, Dad? your going to spend more time with me then .

"Yes, baby, I promise, I will." He returned the kiss and told her, "Come on, baby, buckle up. It's dangerous to drive around without a seat belt."

"Sure will, Dad." Casey continued to buckle up, turned the radio on. She didn't turn the music on too high. Just high enough to put her to sleep. As Casey fell asleep, Michael changed the station and listened to his country station all the way to his place. As soon as he arrived, he carried Casey in to the house. At that point, he had realized how big she had gotten. The last time he had carried her to bed, Casey was around six or so.

He put her down in her room tucked her in gave her a good night kiss an continued to unload the car. Once he had put everything away in her room, he headed to the kitchen, got himself a beer, and headed to the patio. Once he was there, he would stare at the stars for minutes at a time. He had a lot of stuff in his mind. He knew he was living his best moments as an undercover agent. He had just met someone after being a few years alone. He now had Casey, who he was ready to spend some precious moments with. He also thought about the promise he had made to Casey.

He knew the only way to be able to spend more time with her was to give up his job as an undercover agent. That was going to be his priority once he went back to work. He knew from the start the captain wasn't going to be happy about it. But if there was one man who knew him very well other than his dad, that would be the captain. It was a bit late. He finished his beer, took a quick shower, and headed to bed. He knew he had a long day ahead of him tomorrow.

CHAPTER 8

Time with Casey

IT WAS TUESDAY MORNING FIVE minutes shy of 7:00 a.m. Michael's alarm had rung a few times already, but he had hit the Snooze button a few times. By the time he got up, Casey was already in the restroom doing her hair. Good morning, Dad. You're finally up. I went to your room when I woke up, but your snoring got louder and louder. I figured I would let you sleep a bit more while I got ready."

"Good morning, baby. Thanks for the few more minutes of sleep. I really needed them. Be ready in thirty minutes. We will be going out for breakfast while we decide or come up with a plan on where we will be staying while you attend school."

"Sounds good, Dad. I am almost done with my hair. Will dress up a bit after and head out. Can we do IHOP for breakfast, Dad, please, pretty please?"

"Baby, your wish is my command. You requested IHOP, and IHOP it will be." Michael continued to the restroom. As he was brushing his teeth, he got a text message. He headed to the nightstand where he had left his phone. As he had hoped, it was Sally indeed . "Good morning handsome heading to work already hope you have a great day."

That morning text had brought a smile to his face and a lovely feeling of joy. He hadn't felt that feeling in a while. He was really enjoying the moment. He followed to reply. "Good morning beautiful today is the start of my vacations will be having breakfast with my princess you do the same chat with you later."

He got dressed quickly and headed out the door. "Baby, are you ready? I am heading out already. Will turn the truck on and will wait for you at the truck."

"OK, Dad, I am almost done. Give me five." When they arrived at IHOP, Michael asked for a table for two. As they sat down, he asked for a coffee, and Casey got an orange juice. They both asked for a Breakfast Sampler. Casey asked for some Raspberry Peach Pancakes and Michael asked for New York Cheesecake Pancakes. As they waited for their meal, Michael looked at Casey.

"Ok, baby, now is the time to make plans for this whole three months we will be together."

"Well, Dad, what did you have in mind? Didn't you say you had everything planned out already?"

"Well, baby, I had some plans already but didn't remember you still had school to attend. So now we need to add a location near your school to stay, change our weeklong trips to two days as you stated yesterday. If you don't mind, I was thinking about staying at your grandparents' home for the time being. What you think about that?"

"Well, Dad, I was thinking of talking to Mom. Maybe we could stay there at the house Monday through Friday and have the weekends to ourselves. Maybe every other weekend, Mom can come along with us."

"No, baby, that's a no can do. That would never work. Your mom has started dating, and I would feel out of place if she arrived with her date or what not."

Casey just smiled and looked at Michael. "Is that jealousy I hear from you, Dad?"

"No, baby, not at all, just respect. We need to give your mom her alone times and the space she needs."

"OK, Dad. Well, if we got no other option, Nanna and Papa's house will do. I haven't really seen them in a while. This will be a great time to catch up with them and make lovely memories."

"That's my girl."

As they figured their plans out, their meal arrived, and both enjoyed a lovely breakfast. When they finished their breakfast, they both headed toward the truck and started their drive back to Homestead. Michael called his dad just to confirm they would be home when they arrived. His dad answered his call, stated his mother had a doctor's appointment but that they would leave the key in the same place. They always would when Michael was living at home. It was past noon by the time Michael and Casey got to his parents' home. As his dad had stated, they weren't home yet. Michael didn't get all his luggage out just yet. He went around the house and decided to sit out in the back yard as he waited for his parents. Casey was out playing fetch with the dogs. She was having a good time. As she played with them, she remembered that when she was small, she would come out and play with them as well, but back then, the dogs would overpower her and would knock her down at times and would lick her and get her full of drool most of the time.

It wasn't long before Michael's parents got home. They heard all the commotion Casey and the dogs were making, and they knew on the spot they were out in the back. Michael was glad to see his parents. It had been the longest nine months of his life. His dad being a retired officer, he knew the duties Michael had as an officer and didn't mind the time he was away. His mother being married to a retired officer, she had an idea and knew what the feeling was like. She as well was used to that time away from her husband.

Michael's father sat down with him, and his mother went straight to Casey.

"Come on, Casey. Come in and help me make some drinks for Dad and Papa."

"Coming, Nanna. Storm and Shadow don't want me to go yet. We are having a great time together."

"OK, Casey, keep playing with them. Just be careful, honey. While his mother was in the kitchen making some drinks, Michael was out explaining to his father the situation. His dad was a bit too old; otherwise, he was sure he would be jumping for joy when he heard Michael asking to stay at home for a few weeks. As this was going on, his mother walked out with some drinks and noticed the excitement.

"What did I miss? I want to be part of the celebration as well."

As she approached, Michael's Dad gave her the great news. To her luck, Michael was close by; otherwise, she would have dropped the drinks out of excitement.

"Come on, Ma, you got to be careful. You could have gotten injured."

"I will . . . I would have been OK, Michael. It's just part of the excitement."

"So, Ma, what did the doctor tell you?"

"Nothing. Everything was normal. All lab work came back fine, just to keep taking my medication as usual. He gave me another appointment in the next two months."

"That's great, Ma. I am glad to hear that. Now let me get the stuff down, get settled. And how about we go out for lunch?"

"No, sir, we ain't going out for lunch," said Ma. "Well, not on your first night back home, that's for sure. Let me change and I will prepare a homemade meal for you guys."

"Well, Ma, if you're going to put it that way, I won't argue with you. I sure miss your homemade meals. Haven't had them in a while."

While Ma got ready to prepare lunch, Michael went ahead and got all their stuff out of the car. He settled down in his old room and placed Casey's stuff in the guestroom. When he came back, Casey was still out playing with the dogs, and Papa was still out sitting in the patio. Michael sat next to him and asked him if he still had them shotguns and bows they had used so many times when they had both gone out hunting.

Pops just smiled and replied, "I sure do, Michael. They have been waiting for you to use them all this time. What did you have in mind?"

"How about we take Casey out hunting this weekend? I am sure she will love it."

Pops loved the idea. He hadn't gone out hunting in a very long time. The last time he had gone out hunting was when Michael was still married. He had come home for the weekend after one of his undercover jobs and had enjoyed a nice hunting weekend with Pops. Casey had overheard their conversation and didn't like the idea of going hunting just yet. Well, she did like the idea, but it wasn't on her to-do list on her first weekend with her dad.

"Dad, Pops, how about we head out to Disney this weekend? I haven't been out there in a while."

Michael had really wanted to go out hunting, but his priority was to keep Casey happy. "OK, baby, Disney this weekend it shall be."

Casey was excited to hear they would go with her plans. "Dad, if you like, we can go out hunting the following weekend. Now, don't forget we need to go costume shopping as well."

"Yes, baby, costume shopping as well."

While they all made plans for the weekend, Nana came out and called everybody to the dining table. "Lunch is ready, guys. Casey, wash your hands and come and help serve the plates."

"On my way, Nana."

CHAPTER 9

The Arrest

I T WAS SATURDAY MORNING. THE big day to close the undercover case had arrived. It was also the day Casey had chosen to go to Disney World. Michael was up by 6:30 a.m. He was anxious to know what was gonna happen. He knew by 7:00 a.m. that the captain and the whole personnel involved in the arrest for the day would have their morning brief meeting. Everybody would get the basic information about Pedro—all his known locations of where he was last seen, where he lived and whom he socialized the most with.

Michael was really regretting not being part of the arrest now. But he had Casey with him—that was way more important than taking Pedro under arrest. He knew the captain and all the personnel involved would do a great job. He headed downstairs to make a pot of fresh coffee. By the time he arrived to the kitchen, Pops had already beaten him to it.

"Ain't you up super early," said Michael.

"Well, who can sleep with Casey up since 5:00 a.m. or so? She has been walking back and forth from the restroom to her room about twenty times already. Your Ma stated it could be she might be a bit nervous or excited about having a family day at Disney today, and she sure don't have a clue of what to wear."

Michael just smiled at his Pops. "It could be she is hitting her teen years, Pops, what can I say. I just hope the boyfriend issues don't start anytime soon. I sure ain't ready for that yet."

"Oh, they sure are coming, guarantee you that," replied Pops with a sarcastic laugh.

As he headed to his room to get ready, Michael headed to Casey's room to check up on her. As he approached the room, Casey was putting on some lip gloss. She was almost done. She had finally made up her mind on what to wear.

Michael didn't interrupt. He just stood there and watched her get ready. He was just realizing how much Casey had grown at that point. He realized his job had taken too much time away from her. He then knocked on the door and stated, "Good morning, my love, you're looking great today. Be ready by seven thirty, the latest. We will be having breakfast on the road before Ma decides she wants to cook for us."

"OK, Dad, I am almost done. Just doing some final touches on myself."

Michael went to his room, got his keys, and headed downstairs. By the time he was down, Pops had already made him a cup of coffee. Michael got his cup and asked his Pops to follow him to the patio. When they both reached the patio, Michael told him he needed his advice on something. Pops made a confused face, asked Michael what was going on, how could he be of some assistance?

"There's nothing wrong Pops. It's just that I have been thinking a lot. The other day, I made Casey a promise of spending more time with her. My job is taking up too much time away from her. I lost my marriage 'cause of my job, Pops. I don't want to lose her as well. I am afraid if I take another case when I am done with it, she might be in college already."

"You know, Michael, I went through the same situation as you are going through right now. The difference between us was I had the greatest support from your mom. She stood there by my side day in and day out. Yes, we had our ups and downs, at times more downs than ups. But no matter what, she was there for me, especially on those complicated cases. I knew I could count on her for advice or support. I, just like you, missed out on so many great moments of your life. Thank God for pictures and videos your mom would take. Otherwise, I would have lost a lot of precious moments in your life. If you feel it's time to hang the boots, Michael, by all means, you have my support. Don't feel obligated to be an officer just 'cause I was one, Michael. At any point, feel free to make a career change."

"No, Pops, not a career change, not at all. I still want to be an officer. I have been thinking of dropping the undercover job, Pops. Maybe take a homicide job or the gang unit job. Something that won't take my time away from Casey for weeks, months, or maybe years as it has been these past years. I want to know what it feels to come home and enjoy some family time day after day, Pops."

"I had that same feeling you're having right about now, Michael. The difference was I didn't have the courage to leave my job. You do what your heart wants you to do. If you don't, you will lose the passion to serve and protect."

"Thanks for understanding, Pops. I knew I could count on you."

"Don't worry about it, Michael. What's a family for if you can't count on them for support? Now let's hurry up. Your mother and Casey should be ready to go already."

Pops headed to the kitchen to return the coffee cups, and Michael headed to his car. He turned it on so it could warm up. He headed inside the house to hurry up Casey and his parents. Disney World was about four hours away from Homestead. It was past noon by the time they reached Disney World. Michael was anxious to hear the outcome on Pedro's arrest. He wanted to call the captain and get an update on the whole case. He also knew if he called or texted him and interrupted him while in the middle of the arrest, he wouldn't hear the end of it.

As he had made his decision not to interrupt the captain and was about to put the phone away, he got a message from Sally. "I am out on break are you able to talk. If so I am available for 15 minutes. Hope to hear from you."

They had just arrived to Disney World. The line to enter was a bit long. Michael knew he had the time. He had asked his parents to take care of Casey, and he stepped away from them for a while as he made the call. Right after the call, the wait to enter the park wasn't that long. Michael had made up his mind. He had decided the case wasn't going to take priority over his time with his family so he decided to turn his phone off and enjoy a lovely time with them.

It was about 9:00 p.m. by the time they decided to leave the park. As they were walking to the car, Michael turned his phone on. He had several texted messages, a few from Sally and Stephanie. He also had a missed call. He dialed out to retrieve his voice mail. It was from the captain, the voice mail said.

"Michael, we need to speak. Call me back as soon as you get this message."

Michael knew on the spot something bad had happened. If the operation had gone out great, the captain would have said so on the message. The feeling wasn't great. Michael had the urge to call the captain right on the spot. But he knew he still had that long drive home. If he did receive bad news, he wasn't gonna be able to take it on his way home. So Michael decided the call could wait. He followed to read Stephanie's text. It only said she missed Casey. He wanted to talk to her, if possible.

As they got in the car, Michael gave Casey the phone. "Your mom misses you already, baby. Give her a call." It was past 2:00 a.m. by the time they got back home. He helped Casey up to her room. He didn't carry her this time. He remembered how much she weighed and how hard it was to carry her to her room the last time. After he placed her in her bed, he headed outside to call the captain.

"Captain, this is Michael. Called you right back as soon as I got your call. Sorry to call you this late."

"Don't worry, Michael, I am still up. Just wanted to let you know it didn't go as we had wanted."

"What do you mean, Captain? Care to explain?"

"He got away, Michael. We underestimated him. He had more bodyguards than the president. We lost two officers and six were injured, not seriously bad. He will be out for a while. We were able to confiscate twenty kilos, and we got twelve of his men and arrested eight."

"How did he escape, Captain? You guys had all escape routes covered, didn't you all?"

"We thought we did, Michael. We don't know if the house had a secret tunnel which he used to escape or he just outsmarted us."

"Dammit, Captain, I knew I should have stayed with you guys till the end. Maybe. Then this wouldn't have happened."

"No, Michael, you didn't have anything to do with this. We just underestimated him. With you or without, it was bound to happen. Take some rest now. Enjoy your vacation. I will keep you posted. Say hi to Casey for me. Have a great one."

CHAPTER 10

He Got Away

A FEW HOURS AFTER THE RAID, Pedro, Pilas, and Yanko and some of the bodyguards were able to get away. Pedro was so pissed off he couldn't put two and two together right at the moment . Pilas and Yanko kept questioning themselves as to who would be able to call the cops on them. Pilas was the first to bring James Summers out.

"What if the guy was really an undercover cop all along and we never realized it?"

"Don't say stupid shit like that, Pilas. Thanks to that man, I am here with you guys. Besides, the raid was done at our stash house, not our meetup location."

"Someone must have sold us out, boss. There's no way they could have been on to us. The cops were waiting for us. Like if they knew where we were gonna meet up with the load. The bad thing about it is we lost the freaking load as well. I lost all of my men," Yanko stated.

"So did I," replied Pilas. "Hope the damn cops don't work deals with our men they arrested and they rat us out like most of them once they hit jail."

"Look, guys, stop talking shit right now. You guys are just making it worse for me at the moment. We will not move for no reason from this place. The streets are kind of hot today. They must have most of the force out looking for us right as we speak. Thank God for the two cops working with us. They were working on that operation. Otherwise,

I don't think we would have made it out. And if you guys feel James had anything to do with it, those two guys we have on the force would have said something by now, so it can't be James who sold us out . The sad part is I lost my phone there's no way we can stay in contact with the outside world for now."

Pilas was lucky he still had his and had full charge as well. Here you go boss you can use mine . Thanks a lot Pilas, you're the man. Let me make a phone call and we will take it from there.

As Pedro walked away, he tried calling James Summers but had no luck. He tried again and still had no luck. He had no other choice but to send him a text message. He then proceeded to call one of the two officers he had on his payroll. Pedro wanted to know what they were doing with the men that got captured. The cop had informed Pedro that so far they had three being questioned so far out of the three. One looked like he wasn't going to take it and might say more than what he had to."

He also informed Pedro the man they were looking for was just him. Pilas and Yanko were good to go.

"Thanks for the information, keep me posted. As Pedro hung up, he turned around, and directed his conversation to Yanko and Pilas.

"OK, guys, I have just been informed they are on the lookout for me, not you guys. Also, we need to do something about the men that got captured. Based on the information I got, a total eight of our men got captured. The rest got killed. One of them is at the point of saying more than what he needs to say. We don't need that right now. My source will send me an email of the eight that were captured. You guys know your people very well. Once I give you the names of the eight captured, you two will gather more men and head over to their homes and kidnap one family member for each one of them that got arrested. The person in charge of the operation is named Captain Ross. Once you've kidnapped one of their family members, you take them all over to Suri's home. He knows what to do with them."

Suri was the man the cartel would use to disappear people the cartel didn't need anymore. Suri had some tanks full of acid, and he would use them to do the job for him. Once they had someone he had to disappear, he would have them dismembered, and body part by body part, he would get rid of them.

"But you won't do nothing to them until I give you the order."

"Yes, boss," replied Pilas and Yanko, and both headed out of their hiding place and left the location. Pedro made another call. He called his lawyer this time. Ventura was the best lawyer money could buy in Miami. He had been working with the Reynosa cartel for years now.

"Ventura, it's me, Pedro. I need you to head down to police station in the next thirty minutes. I will be getting an email of all my men who got arrested. I have information one is about to say more than what he needs to say. I need you to go in, lawyer them up, and let them know they need to plead the Fifth Amendment. Tell them not to worry. If they play this out right, we will take care of them. If not, they know me very well. They know what might happen. You inform them I will be kidnapping one of their family members as my insurance. Anyone talks, they all die. If they all keep their mouth shut, I will release them all, understood?"

"I will let them know," responded Ventura.

"Get with Pilas and Yanko. Tell them to bring me some food and clean clothing. I will stay hidden for tonight. Pilas and Yanko know where I am at."

"Sounds good. I will head out and wait for your list of members in jail."

After he hung up with Ventura, Pedro got the email he was waiting for. He went ahead and forwarded that information to Ventura and instructed him to forward the information to Pilas and Yanko. They knew what to do with it.

Pilas and Yanko took close to two hours to get back. They brought Pedro a clean change of clothes and some food. Pedro had plenty of time to plan out what he was gonna do. He had lost a big shipment. This wasn't gonna look good on his end. He knew as long as he took care of business and showed them who was in charge, the Big Boss wouldn't make a big deal over it. Pedro questioned Pilas and Yanko over the orders he had given them earlier.

"Boss, we recruited our men as you requested. We left them instructions. They should be able to gather all the people within the next hour or so," replied Yanko .

"Excellent," stated Pedro. "Let me call Suri and give him his instructions. You guys don't leave yet. I have more work for you guys. As soon as the nightfall comes, I am getting out of here. I can't take it anymore. I am going crazy in here."

"I bet you are," replied the guys.

As Pedro changed and ate his food, Pilas and Yanko kept in touch with their guys as far as how many people they had rounded up yet. When he was finished eating, he called Ventura and asked him if he had made contact with all eight men already. Ventura informed Pedro he had indeed gotten in contact with all eight of them already, and all agreed to stay quiet for now. Their only question was, "Pedro, if they have to do time, will the cartel take care of them for as long as they're in jail?"

Pedro didn't have to think about that one. Those eight men hadn't been the only ones that had gone to jail defending the Reynosa cartel. All that had touched jail had been well taken care of till they got out, as well as their families.

Pedro informed Ventura, "You let them know they will each get four hundred dollars a month on their commissary account. As far as the family goes, they won't get the same amount as they were making out here. But we'll give them 50k for every year they get. Now the catch is this: you let them know we will give them the money in one lump sum. If they burn it quick, they won't get any more, that's it, that's all they are gonna get. It's best to save some and slowly use it as they need it. You let them know if one talks, the kidnapped family member will die on the spot and nobody get a dime from us."

"I will let them know, Pedro. Will keep you posted."

After he hung up, Pedro called up the contact he had in the force. "You had stated the person in charge of the operation was a man by the name of Captain Ross, correct? Well, your job will be this: I need you to get me his personal information. I want it all—address, name of wife, how many kids, what he drives, you name it, I want it. I am going to show him how much twenty kilos are worth to me. Get back with me when you get the information. When you get all that, my lawyer will get with you. He will give you something I have set aside for you guys. Keep up the great job."

When he was done with the call, it was starting to get dark. Pedro knew it was time to leave his hideout. He was tired of being there.

"Guys hope you all don't have anything planned for tonight. I want whatever men we have left ready to go in two hours. I have another important job we need to take care of."

"Another job, boss? And what would that be?" asked Yanko.

"You know that man in charge of the operation? We are gonna pay him a visit tonight. We are gonna show him who's boss and who runs the show around here."

"Sure will, boss. Any location we need to head to first?"

"Yes." Pedro requested, "Let's head home. We need to put some money aside for those men in jail. Once we do that and get all the men ready and I get all the information I need, we will head out and have some fun."

It was past midnight by the time Pedro got the address of Captain Ross. Pilas and Yanko had gotten a good lump sum of money set aside to be distributed to the families once they knew how many years their guys were going to get. Three trucks full of armed men headed out with Pedro. It was an hour's drive to get to Ross's home. It was close to 2:00 a.m. by the time they reached his home. When they arrived, Pedro gave them strict instructions. He wanted all family members captured alive. If anybody was going to die, he would do the killing, not anybody else.

They all got off, and Pedro directed everybody where they would be headed to.

As Captain Ross was on his phone, he heard some noise in the backyard but assumed it was a cat or a dog an didn't make anything out of it and walked back to the same spot he was at. As he was about to sit on one of his lawn chairs, he was surprised to see a man pointing a gun to his head and requesting him to hang up the phone. As he did as he was instructed, his hands were trapped and he was blindfolded and rushed to a van. Inside the house was Ross's wife; she as well was abducted and taken as well. As they headed to an abandoned warehouse, Captain Ross was brought down and tied down to a chair with a spot-shining to his face straight to his face. Due to low visibility he wasn't able see no one's face only hear their voices. He heard foot steps approaching then he felt a hard smack on his head. You think your so powerful cause you confiscated my drugs . Who gave me up asked Pedro. Captain Ross just looked away nobody did you brought this upon yourself. Don't play stupid with me old man if you don't want to give up your informant . I have a way that I will make you speak. As he made that comment he made Yanko a sign to bring in his back up plan. As Yanko walked in with Captain Ross wife Pedro pointed the spot light to his wife. You recognize this lady asked Pedro. As Captain Ross was able to get visibility once again he was able to see his wife with Yanko. He tried to struggle and hopefully get loose but his attempt was useless. Calm down old man if you do as your told nothing will happen to her. You took something from me and I want it back. That's impossible what we took from you is already in the evidence room at the station. Theirs no way I will be able to get it back for you. That's your problem not mine stated Pedro. You want your wife back you will have 48 hours to get what you took from me. If we don't hear from you in 48 hours she will die then we come looking for you.

CHAPTER 11

The Call

VERYBODY MUST HAVE BEEN TIRED after a long day at the amusement park. It was around 8:00 a.m. when some commotion in the kitchen woke Michael up. When he checked his phone, he noticed a morning text from Sally. She was dropping by to wish he was enjoying his time with Casey. Wished him a great day, and that she was headed to work already. He went to the restroom and washed his face and brushed his teeth. Then he headed over to Casey's room. She was still sound asleep. Michael felt he would let her sleep a bit more. Besides, it was Sunday after all.

As he was heading downstairs he noticed his Ma was the only one up. He asked his mother where his Pops was at, and she stated he was out doing some chores. Michael headed back upstairs, took a quick shower, and headed out to look for Pops. He told him he would be heading out to Dick's to purchase some missing items to take Casey out fishing. Casey was still asleep. He asked his Pops if they would mind looking over Casey until he came back.

"Not at all. Take your time and go get some good gear 'cause I sure haven't gone out fishing in a while, and I want to go as well."

"Sure will, Pops. Be back in a bit." His whole plan was to head out and see Sally. Having Casey around wasn't going to give him too much time to see her. So he had to take advantage of every free time he had. He remembered the dropped call he had from the captain the night before, so he decided to call him back. The captain didn't answer until the third time Michael called him.

"Captain, you busy?" asked Michael.

"Not at all, Michael," replied the captain. "Just running some errands. Still doing some paperwork over that case from yesterday."

"I see that case still giving you a hard time, Captain."

"Somewhat, Michael, somewhat."

"Is everything OK, Captain? I can tell by your voice there's something bothering you."

"No, Michael, nothing I can't handle. Just some little hiccups here and there."

"Well, all right, boss, if you need anything, don't hesitate to give me a call."

"I have been thinking about it, Michael. When push comes to shove, I will have no other option, and you will be my last resort."

"There you go again, boss."

"Don't listen to me, Michael. You know me, I ain't a morning person."

"Well, boss, have a great one. I am almost at my destination." Michael had decided to stop at Starbucks to get two coffees—one for him and another for Sally. He knew she was working, but he was sure she would find a way to enjoy it. As he walked in to Dick's, he asked at customer service if Sally was working. The lady at the front desk pointed him to register 4.

As he walked over, she was just getting her box and register ready. She didn't have any customers yet. As every Monday, they would have their morning meetings about sales for the weekly expectations and so on. She had her surprised face on when she saw Michael. The coffee had hit the spot. She had woken up a bit late and didn't have time to stop and get one herself. She thought the visit was sweet. She knew she was on the clock. She couldn't chat away as she wanted .

"Are you going to stay for a while? I get an hour for lunch at 11:30 a.m."

Michael just stared at her for a while. He couldn't stop admiring her. That look, that smile mesmerized him.

"Michael, yes or no. Lunch at eleven thirty."

"I am sorry. I was just admiring you. Yes, I love the idea. I am going to stick around for a while. I am going to get some items I am missing for our fishing trip we are having later on today."

"OK, well, meet you just outside the store at eleven thirty, then."

"Sounds good," replied Michael.

As she got her first customer, Michael went his way and started his shopping. He had about two hours to kill before they went out to eat. As he was doing the shopping, he got a text from Casey.

"Hey dad were you at I just got up and you ain't around."

Michael texted her back: "getting some items for our fishing trip later on today baby. You were sound asleep I didn't want to wake you up. Be home in a bit. Ok Dad Lumu she replied.

Michael took his time, got what he needed for his fishing trip, and met Sally at eleven thirty as she had stated. They headed out to Olive Garden over by Park Plaza. They chatted away and enjoyed their meal. Sally told him her day off would be this Saturday. She would love to spend the day with him if it was possible. Michael loved the idea. He told her he would try to make it possible. He said his goodbye and sealed it with a hug and a kiss. She went her way back to work, and Michael headed back to his parents' house. He texted Casey, told her to get ready and he was on his way. When he got home, his dad got the gear loaded

"Ready whenever you are, Michael. Your mom packed some sandwiches just in case we get carried away and take longer than expected."

"Sounds good, Pops. Is Casey ready?"

"She's on her way. She was headed to the restroom as we speak."

As they waited for Casey, Michael got a call from the captain. "Michael, you busy?"

"Not at all, Captain. Just getting ready for a fishing trip."

"Sounds like you're enjoying your time off."

"I sure am, Captain."

"Michael, I just need you to understand and listen clearly to what I am about to say."

"I will, but what's going on?"

"Nothing at the moment, Michael, but hell will break loose over the next few days."

"Will it, Captain? What you mean? Care to explain?"

"No, Michael, I can't do too much talking. Just do me a big favor, do not listen or pay attention to what you will hear over the next few days. You know me very well. We have been working together for a while already. Of all men, you're the one and only one I can trust."

"OK, Captain, you're freaking me out. What you have in mind?"

"I can't say much, or I will make things worse on my end. Please don't ask, just listen, OK. Whatever happens, I am gonna need you to take a closer look at everything you see or hear. Things won't be as they might sound or look."

"OK, Captain, you have me worried already. Let me just drop what I am doing and head your way."

"No, Michael, you're on vacation, and you will stay on vacation. Just do as I say. You're my only salvation out of this. I don't want to get you that involved. The less you know, the better."

"Damn, Captain, all this don't sound good. But when will I know when I need to do all this you're asking me to?"

"Michael, you will know when, believe me, you will. Just wait for the call, Michael. Just wait for the call."

"Now you got to go have a great time with Casey. I will be chatting with you at a later time."

"Sure, Captain. Will wait for your call."

As he hung up, Casey was coming out with her sunblock lotion in her hand . "I am ready to go, Dad."

"So am I, baby. Pops, are you ready? Let's go fishing."

CHAPTER 12

The Unexpected News

ONDAY CAME ALONG, AND MICHAEL was still not feeling that great about that last call he had with Captain Ross. He tried calling him several times, and all his calls would go straight to voice mail. He tried texting him as well, but he didn't get a reply. It wasn't until that Friday morning that he got a call from the Homicide Division. That's when his feelings grew worse. He was asked to show up at the station a.s.a.p. He wanted to ask questions, but the voice on the other end just stated, "Michael don't make it worse than what it looks like. Just come in, please."

He spoke to his Pops, gave him the few information he had. His Pops told him to head over to the station, not to worry about Casey. He would pick her up. Michael got ready and started his drive down to Miami. When he got in, he was escorted to the investigation room. It was Officer Ramirez who walked in after Michael and sat down with some papers in his hand.

Michael looked at him and asked, "Can you explain what's going on? Why do you guys have me in the interrogation room?"

"Mr. Brown, I need you to shut up, calm down, and listen 'cause I have a few questions to ask you," said Officer Ramirez.

"I don't have a clue what's going on. All I know is you're full of shit. Just shoot them questions you got for me. I want to get out of here already before you piss me off."

Officer Ramirez just smiled. "I doubt you're getting out."

"What does that fuckin' mean?"

"Mr. Brown, can you tell us what your last call with Captain Ross was about?"

"My last call with Captain Ross—that's none of your business. That's between the captain and me."

"Mr. Brown, Captain Ross was found dead this morning. We found some text messages coming from you on his phone, and your number was the last number he called. That call lasted about ten minutes. Other things happened as well. At the moment, you ain't involved yet. If we find out you are, things will be a bit worse on your end."

"Look, Ramirez, you ain't making yourself any fuckin' clearer, man. You ain't the man I need to talk to. Get your boss in here. That whole issue of the captain being dead—that can't be fuckin' true as well. You want my side of the story, get your boss in here."

As he made that comment, the glass in the interrogation room was banged twice. Ramirez walked out for a minute, and Chief White walked in.

As he sat down, Michael shook his hand and stated, "Chief, please tell me that's all bull. The captain can't be dead. He was doing fine Sunday night when I spoke to him."

As he made that comment, Chief White made a sign. That meant the recording had to stop. The interview was going to be done without a mic as well.

"Michael I wish I could say the captain is alive, but that would be a lie. The situation don't look good on your end, Michael. The captain did some strange things before he passed away. The only person he spoke to was you, and we need to know what you both spoke about."

"Well, Chief, before I say my part, can I know what's going on? What's that situation you keep mentioning but fail to let me know?"

"Tell you what, Michael, I will give you my word. I have known you for so long. You have been one of Miami's greatest undercover officers. Half of these guys don't have a clue who you are, and I sure don't want you to tell them either. You tell me what you know, then, and only then, will I tell you what's going on."

"Sounds good to me, Chief. Well, I have been on vacation since the last undercover operation I was on. Captain Ross gave me the option to be out from the arrest since I had been on the case for nine months. While I was on vacation, I stayed in contact with the captain. It was him who informed me the suspect had gotten away, but he was able to confiscate the twenty kilos of drugs. It wasn't until Sunday night that he called me. He didn't make any sense at all. He wouldn't explain anything at all. All he said was, 'The less you know, the better. I can't get you that involved.' He also told me, 'Don't believe what you see or hear. Things won't be what they seem. If there's one man I can trust, it's you.' Then he followed by saying 'Just wait for the call.' That was the last comment and call he made to me, Chief."

"I am still in shock as well, Michael. When you hear my side, you will have the same thoughts and expression as me. Well, this is the situation: As you stated, he didn't make the arrest, but he did confiscate the drugs. We tested the drug, and sure enough, it was pure cocaine what he had confiscated. We took the drug in, logged it and weighed it. It sure was a bit more than twenty kilos. Well, Monday comes around, all we have left is one kilo in the storage. We didn't find that out till Thursday night, and that was thanks to Officer Ramirez. He was on his way to check out some items from a closed case when he made the report of what he had found out. Well, we checked the video, and sure enough, it was Captain Ross, the one that went in and took all the drugs. It took him a while, but he was able to do it. Once we found out, we head over to his place, and we find him dead. His face full of coke. The coroner stated he overdosed on it. His wife was also found dead. The report stated she died from a blow to the head. Based on how the body was found, she slipped and hit her head, and that caused her death."

"How about the drugs, Chief?" asked Michael.

"We didn't find them. All we found was what was left on the table. And what he had consumed."

"Did you all find any more evidence? It could have been a setup, Chief. There's no way the captain could have done all this alone. Someone must have been helping him."

"I thought the same, but we can't find any evidence telling us otherwise."

"Who's conducting the investigation on the murder?"

"It's being ruled a suicide, Michael."

"Chief, you know he was murdered."

"We don't have the evidences to back up your story. So without it, we will rule it a suicide."

"Who are the officers doing the investigation?"

"On the missing drugs, we have Officer Washington doing the investigation. On the suicide, we have Officer Ramirez doing the investigation."

"Can I get a copy of both reports?"

"Why would you want them, Michael?"

"Just thought I could take a closer look at them, Chief, that's all.

"As much as I would want to, Michael, I can't. You were one of our lead suspects. Just enjoy your vacations. We have great officers. They will do a great job, I assure you that. Can you keep me posted, Chief?"

"How about this, Michael: I give you an overall once we close the case."

"If that's the most I can get out of you, Chief."

"That will do for now. Michael, do me a big favor."

"Yes, Chief."

"Don't leave town, just in case we have more questions to ask you."

"I won't, Chief, if for some reason I have to. I will let you know."

"Sounds good," said the chief. "Have a great day Michael." As they headed out, Officer Ramirez wanted to question Michael himself and instructed him to return to the interrogation room.

Michael was about to give him a piece, but the chief gave him an ugly look. With that, Michael stood back. The chief looked at Officer Ramirez and stated, "No need to. I have already asked all the questions I need. We can go ahead and eliminate Mr. Brown as a suspect. Continue with your investigation."

Michael headed out of the station with all the information Chief White had shared with him. He still couldn't believe what he had heard. He needed someone to talk to. He called his dad, told him to get ready because he was on his way to pick him up. They headed out to a local bar in Homestead.

Pops knew Michael very well. He knew from the start there was something wrong with him. He didn't ask a thing; he waited until Michael told him what he had to say. As they sat down they opted for a table. Michael asked for a Michelob and a glass of water for his Pops. When the beer arrived, he took a chug and started asking his Pops if he had any friends left in the force. His dad told him he still had a few friends still working.

"That's great, do you think they would be able to help if you asked them?"

"Well, how about you tell me why and we can ask them what they can do for us."

Michael explained to him what the chief had told him. He also told him what he believed but was needing the reports to back up his story.

"Well, how soon do you need the reports? It's a bit late right now. How about we wait for the officers to finish their investigations on both ends, then we ask for the paperwork? If I am able to help you, I am gonna ask you to be very careful, Michael. You never know what you might get yourself into. If these people are able to cover a murder like this, can you imagine how much power they have? Imagine the damage they can cause. Don't want you to be in the captain's shoes anytime soon."

"Don't worry, Pops. I promise you, I will be as careful as possible. Just feel the captain was trying to tell me something. The call, as he said, could have been the one I got today. He did state 'just wait till you get the call.' I got it today, now it's time for me to do my job. I owe it to him, Pops."

"I know what you mean. Just be careful. That's all I am asking you."

CHAPTER 13

Clearing Captain Ross's Name

ICHAEL WAS STILL IN SHOCK and couldn't believe Captain Ross was not among the living anymore. What pissed him off the most was the way they wanted to pin the lost drugs on him. And especially mark his death as a suicide, knowing for sure it was a homicide. All Michael needed was the evidence, and that was what he was out to get. He just needed to know where to start.

As far as he knew, keeping in mind the time he had been working under the captain, not once did they have the bad guy get away. On every case, they had the evidence and the arrest. On this last case, they had the evidence but no arrest. Now the evidence was missing, and Captain Ross was dead. It didn't add up. The captain had been one of the finest when out in the field. There was no way they could have done this to him. He never once complained of having issues, especially at home. The few problems he had were case issues that couldn't be resolved. They took a while, but in the long run, they got resolved, and the case was closed, and that was it. So his few problems weren't enough to kill him.

Michael was going to need a list of the paperwork. He was going to ask his Pops to get it for him. He also needed to find evidence to clear this case and to clear the captain's name as well. His first stop was going to be the captain's home. He got with his Pops and asked him to take care of Casey for him while he went out for a while.

"Don't worry, we can do that for you. All I ask is that you be careful, Michael."

"I will, Pops. I will get with you tonight on the information and reports I am going to need".

"Sounds good. I spoke to my contacts at the office. I gave them a heads-up. They ain't happy about the issue as well. They are willing to help if it means clearing Captain Ross's name."

"Glad to hear that, Pops. Be back in a bit."

Captain Ross's home was about an hour's drive from Michael's parents' home. When he arrived, he drove a few times around the area. He just wanted to make sure nobody was still at the home working on the investigation. The captain's home was out in the country. He had a nice three-bedroom country home out next to a lake. The land had been a gift from his parents before they passed away. The captain, if Michael wasn't mistaken, was on his last payment on the home, and he would be debt free. So if they felt he stole the drugs for money, he had no reason to. They had plenty of opportunities to steal money in previous cases and not once did the captain do it. Every money confiscated was bagged an accounted for. Michael slowly walked the perimeter for evidence. He did notice some tire marks and some cigarette butts a few yards from the home. He quickly took some pictures of the tire marks and the cigarette butts. He didn't have any Ziploc bags; he really wanted to take some for DNA evidence. If he could get the DNA from those butts, he would know who was guarding the home. Why were they? That was what he was going to find out.

As he walked in through the patio, he noticed some blood marks on one of the rocks they had as decoration. Once again, he didn't have the tools for DNA, but he went ahead and took some more pictures. As he walked in, he didn't notice any trace of forced entry. It all looked normal. That was a sign that whoever came in must have been a guest, or the captain was waiting for them. As he entered the living room, he noticed the small scratches on the center table. It looked as if it had just been cleaned. He followed to take some pictures of the scratches. He was curious if that was the table used as the murder location. All he knew was the captain had overdosed consuming cocaine. As long as

Michael had known the captain, not once did he ever mention having an addiction to any drug. It wasn't adding up.

He continued to inspect the home. He noticed two tables without a decoration on them. Not a vase, a picture frame, something to make it look a whole lot better than just a pair of tables by themselves. He didn't find anything to show him that furniture had been moved. So with that, he headed upstairs to the bathroom. That had been the place where Mrs. Ross had been killed, or they made it look like an accident.

The chief had stated that she had slipped in the shower and had died from a blow to the head. As he looked at the shower, he saw it wasn't big enough to slip in it and hit herself on the head. Besides, the restroom was equipped with some handles for carefully entering and exiting the shower. Now the sink counter was about four feet away, and so was the toilet. Total opposite direction from the shower. So if she really slipped, all she would have done was bruised or broken her ribs. Nothing big to cause her death. He followed to take some pictures of the restroom as well.

As he came down stairs, he still wasn't comfortable with the whole table issue. He clearly saw how the upstairs was neatly arranged. There were also some tables there, but each had their respective decorations on them. As he slowly inspected the area where the tables were, he noticed some pieces of broken vases and some glass under the couch. Signs that whoever entered the home caused some damage. He took some pictures of that as well. It all pointed to two homicides. Whoever did it cleaned up after themselves, but not well enough.

When Michael had finished inspecting the place, he called his Pops. Once he answered, he told his Pops he was going to need a copy of the ME report on Captain Ross and his wife. Pictures as well of how the bodies were found. He also asked for a DNA kit and, last but not least, a meeting with Chief White as soon as possible.

His Pops was writing it all down as Michael spoke to him. "Let me make my call and let me see what I can do. Will get back with you as soon as I have a response."

He walked in to the kitchen and remembered he needed some Ziploc bags. He wanted to take the butts he found and try to extract

DNA out of them. They would tell him who was out there guarding the captain. After he gathered the butts, he drove away. Ten minutes into his drive back home, he got a call from an unknown number. He was having second thoughts about answering it. He didn't have anything to lose, so he went ahead an answered the call.

It was Chief White calling. Michael, this is Chief White, do you have a minute?"

"I sure do, Chief."

"I need to speak to you. Michael, let's thank God your father is a well-known retired officer. Otherwise, I would have you arrested for interfering with an investigation."

"Chief, I mean no harm, I promise. All I am trying to do is clear the name of Captain Ross, that's all, sir. Can we meet as soon as possible, sir? If so, can you bring the death reports with you? I want to exchange some information I found today. If what I have with me is on the report, I promise you, Chief, I won't interfere with the investigation anymore, and I will allow the officers in charge to continue with their job."

"Just once, Michael, and I am doing this for your father, keep that in mind. Give me an hour. We will meet at my place. I will forward you my address. Will be there, Chief, heading that way." When he got the text, Michael knew his way and drove to the chief's home. When he arrived, the chief was waiting for him. He signaled Michael to the back part of the home. They would have their meeting at the pool house. As they sat down, the chief asked what it was all about.

Michael told him about several pieces of evidence he had found and wanted to compare with the report. He wanted to start with Captain Ross's overdose. All the report stated was that the captain was pronounced dead Thursday at 9:00 p.m. due to cocaine overdose. No signs of foul play or markings on the body. As he read this out loud, Michael got his phone out.

"Chief, what are the possibilities of having another autopsy, but by a different medical examiner?"

"If you give me motive and new evidence, consider it done."

"OK, Chief, first, a picture of the blood outside of the home, in the patio area. I didn't have a DNA kit, otherwise I would have had a swab with blood I found on the scene. If I am not mistaken, the captain should have had a blow to the head, if that's his blood. Now paperwork shows pictures of the table where he was found, face stuffed with coke. Now look at my picture. It's the same table, but with scratch marks. That's a sign the captain was forced to sniff the coke to the point that he died of an overdose. We need to check his fingernails on that as well. Did you bring his wife's death report as well?"

"I sure did, Michael."

"Let me take a look."

As far as the report, information was minimal. It only said she slipped and fell. Cause of death: blow to the head. It was ruled an accidental death.

"Now, Chief, look at this report and take a look at my pictures. Look at the distance of the shower, toilet, and sink counter. They are all a mile away from each other. If she injured herself, the most she could have gotten would have been bruised ribs, Chief. She was murdered as well. I have a feeling you have a dirty cop and a bought medical examiner. There's no way he could have missed all this."

"Damn it, Michael, I got a feeling we are about to open a can of worms with all this. If what you're telling me is true, I will lose trust in most of my men."

"No, Chief, I got a feeling it's just two rotten apples that you have in your unit."

"What do you mean, Michael?"

"Well, Chief, when I was undercover, a suspect made a comment about having two cops on his side. We need to know if those two cops are just working with him or they are working with someone else."

"Are you saying all this is case-related, Michael?"

"It could be, Chief. I am going to need a big favor from you Chief."

"What's that?"

"I collected these at Captain Ross's home. Someone was guarding his home. We both know the captain doesn't smoke. These butts can prove my point as well. Chief, would it be too hard to get a copy of the surveillance video of the day the drugs went missing? I want to take a second look as well. I got a feeling if the Captain did it, he wasn't alone.

That was too many kilos for him to carry alone. Now, Chief, one last favor."

"Another one, Michael?"

"Just one more, sir."

"Go ahead, what's this last favor you need?"

"I need a copy of all the cases the captain has been assigned to."

"I can't, Michael. That's confidential."

"Even just a list of officers on the cases."

"Yes, Michael, that's confidential as well. Where are you trying to go with all this now?"

"Well, Chief, I got a feeling the arrest was a setup as well. I have been working with the captain for years, and you know very well not once has a case gone south like this one did. I regret not being part of it like I wanted, but the captain insisted that I start my vacation. I didn't think anything wrong out of it. So I went ahead, took his word, and didn't show up for the arrest."

"Let me work on all this tomorrow, Michael. I need to find a way to get an autopsy redone on both bodies without raising suspicions on anybody. If what you have found is true, I need to arrest everybody involved as soon as possible, I do need the evidence to back up the story. I will get with you on the video, and I will take a double look at the list of all men involved in each case and do a comparison on each case. Will have an investigator not related to any cases get in contact with you. Have him mark down every new evidence you find . And we will take it from there. Once I get new information, I will be getting in contact with you."

"Will be waiting for your call, Chief."

"Now one thing, Michael."

"Yes, Chief?"

"Don't go around playing cops off the clock. Let us do our job. You're on vacation, stay on vacation, understood?"

"Yes, sir."

CHAPTER 14

They Might Be Watching Us

SATURDAY CAME AROUND, AND MICHAEL was already feeling bad, as it was. He wasn't spending that much time with Casey anymore. By 7:00 a.m., he got a text from Sally. The text said, "Miss you can't wait to see you."

That made Michael feel a bit worse. With everything going on with Captain Ross's case, he had totally forgotten they had a date this weekend. As he was planning out where to take her out on a nice romantic dinner, he got a call from an unknown number.

"Michael Brown?"

"Yes, sir, how can I help you?"

"Michael, I am Officer Sanders. I was instructed by Chief White to get in contact with you over reinvestigating a closed case. Captain Ross's death, to be exact."

"Yes, Sanders, the chief told me he was gonna work on it, but I didn't know it was going to be this fast."

"We can meet up some other time, if you like."

"Oh no, sir. I want to clear the captain's name as soon as possible. I ain't nothing happy how these people are dragging his name through the mud."

"I know what you mean. I didn't know him personally, but as far as I know, he has been a well-respected officer—well, I mean *was*. You know what I mean."

"Yes, Sanders, I know what you mean. How about we meet up at his place in an hour, if you don't mind? We can start there. Sounds good, Brown. Will be there."

As Michael got ready, he went over to Casey's room. She was still in bed. "Baby, get up. You're gonna be late for school."

"Dad, I ain't feeling that great. It's Saturday today. I get to sleep in."

"What's wrong, baby? You want me to take you to the doctor?"

"No, Dad, it ain't that bad, just not feeling that good."

"OK, baby. Tell you what, I am gonna get a bit busy again today, and I am sorry for waking you up. But I am gonna let Papa know to take you costume shopping once you feel better. As soon as I finish with my errands, I will meet up with you, OK."

"Sure, Dad, have a great day." She kissed him goodbye, turned around, and went back to sleep.

As Michael drove to meet up with Sanders, he replied to Sally and told her some stuff had come up with work and he didn't know if he would be done by then. He would keep her posted if the date would happen or not. She replied with, "Ok don't worry miss you."

When Michael arrived at Captain Ross's home, Officer Sanders was already there waiting for him. Sanders introduced himself and headed to the back of his car. He had the same police reports Chief White had already showed Michael.

"OK, Brown, how about we start with Captain Ross."

"You can call me, Michael."

"Well, if that's the case, you can call me Jerry, how about that?"

"Feels way much better," Michael replied. "OK, Michael had made some copies of the pictures he took and handed them to Jerry. "First we have the cigarette butts. I found them over in this area. We all know the captain don't smoke, so these ain't his, I can assure you that."

Jerry used his evidence cone, marked with a *1*, and snapped a picture. He also started a new report and wrote down the log-in number. The cigarette butt was already marked as an evidence an under DNA testing. He also noted that in his report. He also grabbed a red-ink pen and marked the old report with the same information he posted in his new report.

After that, Michael took Jerry over to the bloodstain. Jerry did the same as before, but with the cone #2, and took another picture. He also marked his notes and red-inked the old report. But this time he got his DNA kit and swabbed the floor and labeled it.

Michael next took him to the center table in the living room and showed him the scratch marks. When Jerry was about to snap the picture, they heard some vehicles coming. Michael looked at Jerry and asked him, "Are you expecting any more help with all this? 'Cause you look like you're doing a great job."

"No help needed," Jerry replied. "I am a one-man show today. The chief didn't mention anything about sending more people. He clearly stated to keep it in the down low."

"Well, looks like somebody found out already."

They both took a window and started looking out. They saw two SUVs approaching and counted about three to four men on each. They parked right behind their vehicles. As they got out, Michael and Jerry noticed there were nine men in total. The men shot all four tires on both vehicles.

"Looks like they don't want us to leave," said Michael.

"Looks like we are outgunned and outnumbered," stated Jerry.

"Not really," replied Michael. The captain always said he kept a nice collection of guns in the basement. How about you keep them busy, don't let them get too close. That should give me some time to look for and gather those guns."

"Did he mention any ammo, or he would just mention the gun collection?"

"That's what I am about to find out. Here are my two guns, just in case you run out of ammo. Be back in a bit."

As Michael went downstairs to search the house for the guns, Jerry started shooting at the men from the windows. He had his guns on one side and Michael's two guns on the other side. He wasn't shooting that many rounds. He wasn't sure if Michael was going to find ammo with the guns. It took Michael about ten minutes to come back up.

"Look what I found. Looks like we could be even now."

They both smiled, and each one took a side and started firing away. It sounded like both were having fun.

"One down," yelled Michael. "Oh, damn it, wait, he's still up. Must have gotten him on the leg. Sucker is limping now.

"Let me show you how it's done," yelled Jerry. "Your three o'clock, he's mine." As he said that, he shot three rounds and hit the gas tank and caused an explosion.

Michael turned around and made his remarks. "Really, Jerry, the vehicle was still good. It only had four flat tires."

"It's called being creative," responded Jerry. And both just smiled and fired away, each holding their grounds.

"I got two now," yelled Jerry.

I got one," replied Michael. "Six more to go. They are dividing themselves. Three were going towards the kitchen.

"I got those!" yelled Jerry. He got more ammo and headed toward the kitchen windows. As he started shooting, Michael yelled at him, "Jerry, don't forget once we are done, we got some missing evidence upstairs we have to take a look at as well. We still have more," yelled Jerry.

"Yes, sir, we do," replied Michael. "Jerry, how long you been an officer?" asked Michael.

"Fourteen years. Why the curiosity?"

"Well, I figured I would never find anybody as crazy as me."

"Crazy, how is that?"

"Well, I like to have a few conversations here and there in situations like this. It helps me not to hit that panic stage."

Jerry just smiled. "Well, looks like you have found your brother from another mother, my man. I have the same problem just like you."

"I got another one," yelled Michael. "Five to go."

Jerry said, "Are you thinking what I am thinking about these shooters?"

"No, I don't have a clue what you're thinking," replied Michael.

"You might have a point about the captain's death. What are these armed men doing here? What are they looking for? Who sent them? How did they know we would be here? They did come for us, Michael.

Otherwise, why would they shoot our tires out? They didn't want us to escape. They came with the intention of killing us. Little did they know it wasn't going to happen."

"One more down," yelled Michael. "Looks like they are retreating. My guys are returning to their vehicle!" yelled Jerry.

"So is the one I had left," said Michael. "It's best they leave. We were running out of ammo."

"Absolutely," replied Jerry. "Are you hit?"

"Not at all. I am clean, how about you? I got a little scratch on the right arm, but I will be OK. Those men came looking for something. If not, they came after us. Let me call in the shooting. Then will get in contact with the chief."

"Yeah, you do that. We need answers," said Michael.

As Jerry made the calls, Michael walked out. He wanted to make sure the bodies on the ground were dead. He didn't want any surprises and get shot out of the blue. As he approached the area where the burned body was at, a few feet away, he noticed the same brand of cigarette butts on the ground as the ones left behind and being under DNA testing. "Looks like whoever got off the truck was the same person guarding the captains home the other day. Could it be one of the dead ones or one of the ones that fled away." As he was still looking around for some connection to the case, Jerry was calling him.

"Michael, the chief wants to speak to you."

"Heading your way," replied Michael.

When he took the phone, the chief asked him if he was OK.

"Yeah, Chief, we are both OK."

"Jerry went ahead and gave me the details. Is there any chance they might have left something behind?"

"No, Chief, I don't think that's the case in this situation. Why go through all the trouble of making this look like an accidental death on Captain Ross, make it look like an overdose death?

"These guys were coming for us, Chief. The question is, how did they know we were here? Did you talk to anybody about it, Chief? "Not at all. I did inform Officer Ramirez to hand over the closed-case paperwork if they were ready. I told him Jerry was gonna take a double look at it. I spoke to the person in charge of the forensic report. I placed him on suspension with pay while we're reinvestigating this whole case. I asked him if he had anything to tell me. He said no and walked out."

"That could be it, Chief. He made the call. He must have known you were on to him on what he did. He must have called the person that paid him to falsify the reports. The person he called sent the gunmen to us. Officer Ramirez must have guessed we were out here since you asked him for the reports. It could have been him as well. Chief, can you get a call report from your forensics guy so we can see who he last called right after your meeting with him? And can you do the same with Officer Ramirez's call log as well? We need to see if they have been staying in contact lately."

"OK, I can do that. I am putting the pieces together already, Michael. I am seeing your side of the story. Looks like you might be right all along. We need to find out who has been playing on both sides of the fence. Once we do that, we can get justice for what they did to Captain Ross. And about the list you asked for, Michael is still working on it. Haven't had the chance to look at all the cases yet. I can get the information for you quick, but I don't want to get too many people involved . For now, Jerry will stay with you. If you need anything, he has instructions to assist you by all means necessary."

"Thank you, Chief. It really means a lot." As he hung up, Jerry signaled to him. "Come on, let's check the upstairs restroom. We need to take some additional pictures before the rest of the officers get here. The report states she accidentally slipped and hit her head. Now you said everything was too far away apart there was no way she would have struck her head. Just a little heads-up, I don't know if the chief told you, but he has ordered a new autopsy on Captain Ross and his wife."

"Good. Looks like the truth is finally gonna come out," stated Michael. As they took pictures and Jerry wrote down notes on his reports, the officers arrived. They each showed Michael and Jerry their officers' credentials and took down their reports of what had happened. Michael ordered them to take the cigarette butts for DNA. He requested them to be matched with a different case Jerry had been working on.

CHAPTER 15

Spending Time with Casey and Sally

S SOON AS THE OFFICERS were done with all the investigation, they informed Michael he was OK to leave. At that point, he realized he didn't have a vehicle. Thanks to Jerry being so creative, he was now without a vehicle to move. Jerry noticed his facial reaction and just smiled.

"Will you be walking, or would you like a ride?"

"A ride would be OK, but keep in mind, I sure ain't helping you change any tires."

"We ain't changing any tires. They are picking up both vehicles for now. I will be getting a backup one. Tomorrow you can stop by the office. The chief will be issuing you a new one."

"Just take me home, man. I have had enough action for one day."

When he got home, Casey was already up and doing some chores with Papa out in the barn. She was feeling a whole lot better, and she was ready for some Halloween costume shopping. She ran upstairs to change and get ready. He asked his Papa and Nana if they wanted to join them for an evening out. Plans were to get a costume for Casey and take her out to eat as well. They didn't have any plans, so they both decided to tag along. As they drove to Miami, Michael got a WYD text from Sally. He hadn't spent time with her either. With everything going on, he couldn't spend too much time with Sally or Casey. Clearing

Captain's Ross name was taking too much time away from him. But he knew it was well worth it.

He was thinking about having Sally tag along. He thought it was a bit too early, but he had no other choice if he wanted to spend time with her. While he drove he asked Casey how she felt if he would start dating. She made a sad face but knew it was soon to happen. All she asked was to keep her in the loop, not to hide away and all of a sudden come out with a wedding invitation. Michael just laughed about the comment.

"Not at all, baby. That's too soon. I know for now she's the one I want to spend time with. Get you involved and see how both of you get along. Now, she has kids as well. We need to keep that in mind as well. So if you guys don't mind, I wanted to invite her to eat with us today. What do you all think?"

"We are OK," said Papa and Nana.

"How do you feel about it, Casey?" asked Nana.

She was just looking out the window while she responded. "I am OK with it if you feel she's the one, Dad."

"Great! Thanks, guys. Let me let her know. He went ahead and texted her. "Meet me at Olive Garden by Park Plaza I have a surprise for you. Can't wait to see you. Will stop by the Halloween store over by Flagler street 1st. That should give you some time to get ready."

"Ok see you there," she replied.

As soon as they arrived at the Halloween store, Casey went crazy. She had so many options to choose from. It had been so long since she had spent Halloween with her dad. Her idea was to pick a costume that would involve her Dad as well. At first, he didn't like the idea. He must have felt the guilt kicking in because at the end, he agreed. In the end, they came out with two costumes. Casey was gonna wear the Little Red Riding Hood costume. She looked gorgeous in it. As for Michael, he would be playing the Big Bad Wolf for this Halloween.

After he paid and they walked out of the store, he texted Sally. "We are on our way."

She replied with a "WE? What do you mean."

He replied, "my bad I am on my way. See you there."

When they arrived, Sally wasn't there yet. He got a table for five and ordered some drinks. When she arrived, she sent him a text. "Meet me at the door."

He excused himself from the table and headed to the door. As she walked in, he received her with a hug and a kiss.

"So where is that surprise you talked about?"

Michael just smiled. "Remember when I told you I wanted to take you serious. And getting to know you meant a lot to me. So I decided to have you meet the family."

As he said that, she turned around and walked out of the restaurant. He followed her out and called her back. She didn't walk far. As she turned around, Michael noticed she had teary eyes.

"What's wrong? What did I do this time?"

"Nothing wrong. It's just me. I am so emotional. I am glad you left your credit card behind that day. I am a strong believer when I say everything happens for a reason. I have been hurt in the past. I will give you all my trust, just promise me you ain't gonna let me down."

Michael gave her a big tight hug and followed it with a kiss. "If my intentions weren't to take you seriously, I wouldn't have invited you to this family dinner. If you're gonna be part of this family, now is the time to meet them."

Sally wiped her face and walked right back in. She told Michael she would head to the restroom first. She would meet him at the table. As he walked right back in, Casey asked him what happened.

"She didn't make it, did she change her mind?"

"No, baby, she went to the restroom. She should be out in a bit."

As he said that, Casey asked to be excused. She, all of a sudden, had the urge to use the restroom as well. Sally and Casey took a while to come back. Michael asked Nana if she would mind checking up on Casey.

Nana headed to the restroom as well. A few minutes later, all three of them came out smiling and laughing. Michael felt a good feeling knowing Casey and Nana were getting along with Sally. As she sat down, Michael introduced her to Papa.

"As you might already know, this is my mother, and she is Casey."

"Yes, I met them in the restroom. They are so sweet. Mr. Brown, nice to meet you as well."

Once they got the meet-and-greet out of the way, they went ahead and ordered their meal. While they waited, Michael and Sally ordered a drink. They all chatted the night away while they waited. Casey insisted that she wanted to know how many kids she had and their ages.

"It ain't cause I want to be nosy, but honestly, I have always been an only child. I have never had the pleasure of spending holidays with other children. As you might know, I will be spending this Halloween with my father. I will be Little Red Riding Hood, and he will be the Big Bad Wolf. If you, Dad and Sally don't mind, Halloween is a few weeks away. Maybe we can all spend it together, her children and us. That means more costume shopping."

Michael and Papa and Nana were surprised how Casey was reacting. They assumed she was gonna take it hard, assuming she still wanted her parents to get back together. Over all, Michael loved the idea.

"Well, baby, we would need to see how Sally feels about it. We are OK, but why don't you ask her."

Sally stayed quiet for a while. "Let me chat with my kids, let them know about you guys. Maybe we can have dinner next week. You guys come over and we take it from there."

"Excellent," said Casey. "We can't wait."

Michael was still in shock over Casey's reaction. He replied, "Yes, baby, we can't wait."

When dinner arrived, they all started enjoying their meal. Halfway through his meal, Michael saw four men walk past their table. He thought he recognized two of them, but at the moment, he couldn't remember from where. He was really enjoying the family time that he didn't worry about it. All four men walked out of the restaurant in the direction of the alley.

Then all of a sudden, inside the restaurant, everybody heard four shots coming from outside. Michael's first instinct was to get up and reach for his gun.

"I have a responsibility as an officer. Hope you guys understand."

"Just be careful," they all said.

As he was about to walk out, he handed Sally his phone. "Search for Jerry in my contacts. Let him know what's going on. Let him know I will be waiting for him."

As he walked out, he saw the store manager by the entrance, and he showed him his badge. "Get all customers to the back part of the restaurant. Tell your employees not to open the back door for no reason, and dial 911."

He walked out with caution and headed to the alley. He saw the four men two with guns out and the other two kicking two bodies on the floor. One kept on asking for his payment, or all would encounter the same luck as the one that was already dead.

Michael knew he didn't have a lot of time to wait for his backup if he wanted to save the other two. He had no choice but to attempt to do something about it. As he walked into the alley, he showed his badge and ordered everybody to put their guns down. As he pointed his gun, the two men responded with bullets. Michael took cover but responded right back. As he shot some rounds, he took one guy down and badly injured another. He took cover again to avoid being hit. Then he once again fired some more shots and took one more guy out.

As he was about to take cover, the remaining man yelled out, "Don't shoot! I surrender."

As Michael walked out to disarm him, he noticed he had his gun pointed at his head. "If you move, I will kill myself."

Michael tried to talk him out of it, but he wouldn't listen. All of a sudden, Michael heard someone scream.

"Officer Ramirez with the Miami Police Department, put your guns down."

Michael turned around and flashed him his badge. "We are on the same team. Got one pointing his gun at his head, won't surrender."

"I got this," he said.

Michael didn't know if he was the meanest, toughest cop, or just the dumbest one of them all. He went ahead and put his gun away and walked straight over to the man. His whole way toward him, he spoke Spanish to the man. Not once did the man with the gun respond.

As soon as Ramirez was ten feet away from him, the man decided to end his life and shot himself in the head. Officer Ramirez turned around and stated, "I almost had him."

Once they exited the alley and got some light on each other, he took out his phone and sent out a text message. Then he gave Michael the longest stare he had ever received.

"You're the guy I had in the interrogation room on Captains Ross's case."

"Yes, sir, that was me," Michael replied.

"No wonder I couldn't find you on our database. Your information would come out blank, and that's because I tried it several times. Are you special ops or Navy SEAL, what's your story?" he asked. "What division do you work for."

"Just a traffic stop officer, that's all," Michael replied. "Would you care to explain what exactly did you say to that man that just shot himself?

"I had it under control. I could have gotten him alive out of this one."

"Well, don't worry, he's gone now. No need to sweat over it. So what did you and the chief talk about once the mic was turned off?"

"Nothing important, no need to sweat over it," replied Michael. As he made that last comment, the first crew of backup showed up. They reported to Michael, and he instructed them to close the perimeter. He also informed them there were two survivors in the alley, to get their statement and information and wait for forensic and investigators to do their part. As he finished, Jerry showed up and headed straight to him.

"Is everything OK? I heard the call over the radio."

"Hey, look at the bright side. Just one car arrived before me. Wait, did Ramirez make the call he had arrived at the scene?"

"Ramirez is here as well?"

"You bet he is. He arrived first. He walked straight to the last guy, pointing a gun to his head. Spoke Spanish to him all the way. He was ten feet from him when the poor man shot himself."

"Did Ramirez say what he told him before he shot himself?"

"Nope. He said not to sweat over it. And he changed the subject on me."

As they were both discussing the death of the last man, Ramirez showed up. "Officer Brown, we need to talk."

"Well, whatever you need to say, you can say it in front of Jerry. He's a man I trust with my life."

"Well, if that's the case, let me tell you that you just didn't kill any John Doe in the alley. Based on the identification I was able to retrieve from them, one of the dead bodies is the son of El Checo, the Reynosa cartel's main boss. Once he finds out, I can assure you he'll will break loose here in Miami. We need to find out what he was doing here in Miami."

As soon as he finished making those comments, a black SUV drove by and shot three full rounds of what seemed to be AK-47s. They all took cover. It all happened so fast that they didn't have time to react.

As the shooters drove away, Jerry quickly ran to his vehicle to call in the shooting and put out a *bolo* on the black SUV heading south of Olive Garden.

Once they got control of the area once again, they noticed the officer placing the police tape on their crime scene had been killed. An innocent bystander looking around was killed as well. Two customers inside Olive Garden were badly injured. Michael ran inside to make sure his family was OK. Once he confirmed everybody was OK, he guided them toward the exit.

"Looks like we can leave already, guys."

Once they were outside the restaurant, Officer Ramirez stopped Michael and his family.

"Sorry, buddy, nobody can leave just yet. I have ordered the officers to take everybody's statement. Especially those that were in the restaurant at the time of the shooting. After the statement, we will be taking some pictures as well with all their information, just in case we need to get back with them."

"Pictures? Are you serious?" asked Michael.

Jerry placed his hand on Michael's shoulder. "Just let the man do his job, please.

"OK, won't argue with you on this one, Jerry. I will be waiting for you guys in the car," said Michael to his family.

As he was about to walk away, Ramirez stopped him. "Officer Brown, I need your version, and picture as well. You were eating as well when the shooting occurred."

"My information? Are you freaking kidding me, Officer Ramirez?"

"Officer Brown, were you eating here or not? If so, be patient and pose for the pic."

CHAPTER 16

Right Before the Shooting

P EDRO GOT TOGETHER WITH JUNIOR over some deal not paid yet. Junior was the oldest child of El Checo, the leader of the Reynosa cartel. His plans were to gain control of Miami and gain more power. For that he chose Pedro as his main contact in Miami. He would have Junior help him out and learn from it. Just in case he would take charge of the Reynosa cartel one day.

Pedro had a deal a few days ago. The person he sold the drugs to had agreed to pay him that same day. Twenty-four hours had gone by, and they still hadn't heard from him. Pedro got a call from Officer Ramirez; the call was to inform him the person that owed him money was about to enter Olive Garden with some friends. Pedro instructed him to wait outside and follow him just in case he left. Not to move unless he got other instructions from him.

As he got this call, he was discussing with Junior about going over to collect his money. Junior had wanted to make a name for himself and told Pedro he would go instead. It was time he showed his father he could finally take charge of the business one day.

Pedro had other plans a few blocks away from Olive Garden, so he decided to give Junior a chance. As they both agreed, Pedro instructed three men to head out with him. When he arrived, he met up with Officer Ramirez. He instructed him not to get involved and to serve as backup just in case things didn't go as planned.

Junior and the men that went with him waited in their vehicle for a while. Junior got tired of waiting and ordered all men to get off with him. They all headed in to the restaurant to find the people they were looking for. Once they made contact they instructed them to meet them by alley beside the Olive Garden. Once they got there, he instructed one of them to wait by the door. Once the man they were waiting for would come out, he was to direct them to the alley.

A few minutes had passed by. Junior and the men were lucky the man they were waiting for was already heading out. As they stepped out of the restaurant, Junior's man was waiting for them. He flashed them his gun and ordered them to follow him to the alley. As they arrived to were Junior was at, Junior ordered the men not involved to be separated from their man. Junior had a one-on-one talk with their man. He demanded his money, and he wanted his money right away.

The man didn't give him the answer he wanted to hear. Because right after his comment, Junior and one of his men gave him the beating of a lifetime. One of his friends tried to interfere to help him out. At that point, Junior knew he wasn't gonna get his money. He pulled his gun out and shot the man and his friend. As he was about the kill the other two, Officer Michael Brown showed up and ordered everybody to put their guns down.

Junior and his men had no other option but to shoot their way out. They fired a few rounds at Michael but had no luck. Michael took cover behind a big metal trash container. As he fired his first rounds, he got one and badly injured another one. As Michael took cover, Junior called Officer Ramirez for backup.

Michael took another chance and fired some more rounds. As he fired away, he hit Junior an killed him. As there was one man left, he surrendered and yelled to cease fire but kept his gun pointed at his head. Michael came out from behind the trash can. As he attempted to have the man put his gun down, Officer Ramirez showed up, but at that point, it was a bit too late. He presented himself upon Michael, but Michael showed him his badge. Michael told him about the man with the gun pointed to his head. At that point, Officer Ramirez put his gun away and walked toward the man.

"Que ases baboso si ya estás muerto." (What are doing, you dumbass, if you are already dead.) "Saves lo que te va ser el patrón si te entregas?" (Do you know what the boss will do to you if you turn yourself in?). "Si cabron te matará a ti y a toda tu perra familia por no defender al Junior." (Yes, sucker, he will kill you and your whole family for not protecting Junior.) "Dime que vas a ser te matas solo oh te desaparesemos a toda tu familia." (So tell me, what are you gonna do, kill yourself, or we disappear your whole family?)

After that last comment, the last man alive took his own life. After he killed himself, Officer Ramirez walked back to Michael and Michael asked him what he had done. The man was about to turn himself in. He also asked Officer Ramirez, "What did you tell him?"

"Don't worry, he's gone now, no need to sweat over it." Officer Ramirez had no option but to text Pedro of the bad news. And send him the address of the location. Before they knew it, Pedro drove by and took care of business. To his luck, he killed some people, but not the officer he had wanted. A few miles away, they burned the vehicle and fled away in a different one. He once again texted Officer Ramirez.

"If we couldn't get the job done, I want you to get me all the information on that son of a bitch. I want him dead as soon as possible."

CHAPTER 17

Time to Protect the Family

AS SOON AS EVERYBODY HAD made their statements and had their picture taken, they all got together and headed to the vehicles. Sally and Casey were the ones affected the most. Papa being a police officer for so many years made Nana ready for anything. She was a bit shaken, but nothing major. Sally was in no condition to drive. Michael offered to drive her home if she liked. Sally informed him she really didn't like the idea. She didn't have her kids this weekend. She would end up spending the weekend alone. She didn't mind doing so, but after everything that had just happened, it made it a bit worse.

"If you think you won't make it alone tonight, you're more than welcome to stay with us. We can fix a room for you tonight," said Nana. "We can spend it together tonight. We all need the company."

Sally didn't think about it twice and agreed. Papa decided to drive home. He didn't have a clue how to comfort Sally. He didn't have an issue with Nana and Casey. Michael understood his point of view, so he took the back seat with them. Casey fell asleep on his lap and Sally on his shoulders. When they arrived, Sally helped Michael take Casey upstairs. Nana headed to the kitchen and invited Sally to join her. She made some coffee and hot chocolate for them. Michael and Papa took some coffee and Nana and Sally took some chocolate. As the cups were served, they all headed to the patio.

"How you feeling, Sally," asked Nana.

"Still a bit nervous about all this. I have never been through something like this."

"Do you think you can get used to it?" asked Nana.

"Honestly, I do just wish I could be as calm as you are being right now."

"Forty-five years of being married to a retired undercover police officer will do this to you."

"Wow that's a lot of years. Congratulations to both of you. Especially to you, Nana, for supporting him with his career for this long." She then followed to look at Michael and stated, "If you're serious about us and it's gonna last as long as their marriage, I am sure I can get used to it." She hugged Michael and gave him a kiss. They stayed up late chatting the night away about each other's nice moments in life. They each took turns telling something about each other. Once Sally felt she was tired and was OK to fall asleep, they all followed right behind her.

The following morning, Michael's phone was swamped with text messages saying, "Pick up your phone mother fucker."

He didn't recognize the number' he figured it must have been a prank or someone that didn't have anything better to do than cause trouble, simple as that. As he was waking up, Sally and Nana were already in the kitchen making breakfast. Papa was out by the barn, and Casey was still in bed. He got a cup of coffee and followed Papa to the barn. As he walked out in Papa's direction, he got a call from the same number he had been getting messages from all morning.

When he picked up, he heard a familiar voice on the other end.

"Good morning, James Summers. Or should I say Michael Brown?"

When Michael heard this, he moved away from Papa and continued to ask who the hell it was. He had an idea who it could be but wanted the person on the other end to confirm he was correct.

"No te agas pendejo, cabron." (Don't play dumb, sucker.) "You know very well who I am . I brought you in to my home, offered you my trust and friendship, and this is the way you repay me. By taking one of my most precious children away from me? Te vas a morir perro." (You're gonna die, dog.) "I will make you suffer ten times worse than what I am suffering right now. I will not rest until I disappear you. If you get the cops involved, I will continue with your close friends and family as well."

After that, Checo dropped the call.

Michael got his coffee cup and threw it against the barn. Papa rushed to him and asked what was wrong.

"Nothing, Papa. I am gonna need you and Nana and Casey to head to the vacation home you have."

"You want us to head to the cabin, Michael? What's going on? We need an explanation."

"One of the men I killed last night in the alley was the son of a drug cartel boss. I don't have a clue how he got this number. But I am sure just the same way he got this number, he will get this address as well, Papa. I don't want nothing to happen to you guys. Please don't make a big commotion, just say you want to take a short vacation. Take the essentials and head out as soon as possible. I will head out, get us some new prepaid phones and we will not communicate through these phones anymore. Be back in a bit, Papa."

Michael went inside the house, got the keys to the truck, and told Nana and Sally he would be back in a bit. He headed to a convenient store. He bought three phones and returned home. On his way home, he called Jerry.

When Jerry answered, Michael told him, "Don't ask questions, stop what you're doing, and head to the address I am about to text you. We'll chat when you get here."

"On my way," replied Jerry.

When Michael got back, Nana was already getting some luggage ready, and Casey was in the shower. She had loved the idea of going up to the cabin. Michael gave Papa one of the phones and gave him his new number. He did the same to Sally.

"I need you to stop using your phone for a couple of days, please. You will use this new phone from now till I tell you otherwise. This is my number just in case you need to get a hold of me.

"Michael, what's going on? Why do we need to do this?"

"Sally, can you please step outside with me? We need to talk."

As Sally stepped outside Michael instructed her to keep her questions limited. He wasn't able to give her the full details as of that moment.

"Remember how last night you said you would stick with me through thick and thin?"

"Yes, I do," replied Sally.

"Well, OK, now is one of those moments. I am gonna drop you off at your home. You will get the essentials as well for you and your kids and head to your parents or a relative, but I don't want you at your home till you hear from me."

"Michael, please trust me, let me know what's going on. How do you expect to make this work if you're already keeping things from me?"

"OK, Sally I will let you know, but I need you to keep calm. I don't want you to scare or alarm Casey. Last night's situation was enough for her."

"I promise," said Sally.

"OK, well, one of the persons I killed last night on the alley of Olive Garden happens to be the son of a drug lord of a Mexican cartel. He just called me and told me he will be out to get you guys. He wants me to suffer as much as he is suffering. For that I need to get to him before he gets to you guys. And for that, I need to know you guys will be safe before I do anything."

"Oh my god, Michael, what are we gonna do? We need to call the cops."

"Sally . . . Sally, keep calm. I need you to be calm. I can't get nobody involved. He said he would make it worse and go after my friends as well if I do so. I need to keep this on the down low for now. Please do as I say, and everything will turn out OK."

As they were both walking into the house, Michael got a call from Jerry. He answered.

"I am still waiting for the text, my man."

"Sorry, Jerry, all hell just broke loose here at home. You got a pen?"

"No, sir, I don't. I am driving."

"OK, let me text it right now. Will be waiting for you." He sent Jerry the text and walked into the house.

As he was walking in, Casey ran up to him. "It's hunting time, Daddy. Can't wait to hit the cabin. When are we leaving, how long are we gonna be there?"

"Baby, I won't be going with you for now. You will be going with Papa and Nana for now. I will head to the station to pick up my car from the station. Then I will give Papa a call. I am gonna need for you to make a list of what we need to have a great hunting week."

"Week, you said, Dad. How about school?"

"Don't worry, baby, I got that covered."

"OK, Dad, if you say so. Just let Mom know. Otherwise, they will be calling her, and you won't hear the end of it, trust me when I say that."

"OK, baby, I will keep her posted."

"Breakfast is ready!" yelled Nana. "Everybody, come down to eat."

As they all were eating, Jerry arrived and knocked at the door.

"Did I arrive at the right time?"

"You sure did," said Papa. "Any friend of Michael's is a friend of the family."

Nana got up and made him a plate. Jerry followed to sit with everybody at the table. As they all finished, Sally and Nana did the dishes while Casey cleaned the table. Papa went to the basement to get his guns and ammo ready just in case he needed them.

Michael and Jerry stepped outside to speak more in private. Jerry asked him, "What's going on, what's the urgency?"

"Those men I killed yesterday, one of them was the son of Checo, the Reynosa cartel boss. So Ramirez wasn't bullshitting us yesterday when he said that. That SOB, I am also gonna need a meeting with the chief a.s.a.p. Ramirez is one of the two cops working with the cartel."

"How do you know that Michael?"

"Last night in the alley, he said that was the child of El Checo. That man I killed wasn't on any of our reports. He didn't even have a criminal record. There was no way of knowing that just right off the bat. Not before he proceeded with the investigation, I saw him get his phone and send some texts . A few minutes later, a truck showed up, shooting bullets all over the place. Now, that man that shot himself—he was about to surrender. I don't have a clue what Ramirez told him . But whatever he told him pushed him to kill himself. Like if he told him you couldn't protect the boss's son. What makes you think you're gonna live long anyways?"

"Damn, Michael. But Ramirez? Are you serious?"

"Who else could it be? Now I get this call from this motherfucker this morning. Why did Ramirez change his protocol yesterday with all his witnesses? He knew he didn't have any information on me. That was his only way. And me, like a damn fool, I fell for it like an idiot. Now I have placed my whole family in danger. I gave my Papa instructions of where to meet up with him."

"Sounds good, Michael. How about Sally?"

"Well, I was thinking about dropping her off on our way to see the chief."

"Sure, we can do that, it's on our way."

"OK, let me tell Sally. We are ready, and we need to go ."

As they all got in the car, Michael asked Jerry to call the chief and set up a meeting. Once they had dropped Sally off, they headed off to meet up with the chief. Michael gave the chief all the information he had. As he did so, the chief was trying to put two and two together. He was trying to see everything from Michael's point of view. To close it up, Michael told the chief about the call he got.

The chief offered him help and protection, but Michael refused. He told the chief his family was on their way to a hideout. A place nobody knew about.

"That's a great idea, Michael. If you feel we can help you out in any way, don't hesitate to ask."

"I need a big favor, Chief."

"What is that you need?"

"Can you get Ramirez into the office? We need to get as much information from him. He could be our only way to them."

"Let me make a call, but you won't be able to get involved, Michael. We take him in, we do the interrogation."

"Sounds good to me, Chief."

As the chief made the call, the person on the other end told him Officer Ramirez had called in sick. "Can I get an address on him?"

As the chief waited, he grabbed the phone and covered it to let Michael know Ramirez had called in. "But they are about to give me his address. We can pay him a visit. Just to make sure he is OK." The chief asked for a pen and wrote down the address they gave him. "OK guys, how about we pay him a home visit. We could say we are concerned coworkers."

"If you show up asking for him, he's gonna know we are on to him. He could make some calls and let them know you guys know already. That's just gonna make things worse. So if you don't mind, I was thinking me and Jerry could pay him a visit."

"Yeah, you could be right. Whatever happens, you guys be careful, and keep me posted."

"We will, Chief. Thanks for understanding." When they arrived at Ramirez's home, the wife came out and stated he was out working, and followed to ask, "Are you guys investigating that beating some coworker gave him yesterday?"

Michael and Jerry just looked at each other.

"Yes, ma'am, we are. We needed to get Ramirez's point of view over the argument."

"OK, if he calls or shows up, I will let him know."

As they were leaving the location, Jerry noticed two vehicles were parked in the driveway. They assumed one belonged to the wife and the other to Ramirez. So if he wasn't home, there was a possibility he was out driving in his cop car. As they drove away, Jerry called the chief.

"Boss, can you check on Ramirez's GPS. He ain't home. Wife stated he went out to work. He called in he wasn't feeling good. Someone is not telling the truth. Text me the address when you get it."

"Sure will," responded the chief.

"What did the chief say?" asked Michael.

"He's gonna look up Ramirez's location. All police vehicles have GPS now. They know our every move, Michael."

"Yeah, your vehicles, mine have never had a GPS installed. Well, I don't know about this new one I am gonna get, thanks to someone."

Jerry just smiled back at his remarks. "Man, are you ever gonna get over it?"

As Jerry made that statement, he got a call. The chief had Ramirez's location. "Yes, Chief, 300 South Biscayne Avenue. Hmm, ain't those the expensive apartments in downtown Miami?"

"I think so," replied the chief. "I am about to give him a call, let him know you guys are on your way to pick up some information we need from him on an old case. Hope he don't suspect a thing."

"OK, Chief, we are on our way."

When they arrived, they circled the area a few times, just looking for anything out of the ordinary. If they were correct, he was with Pedro or someone with big power. These apartments were too expensive for an officer's salary. As they decided to get off and look for Officer Ramirez, they noticed a man seating at a bench getting his shoes shined. That didn't look bad. What made it look bad was he had the newspaper upside down. They knew on the spot he was looking out for cops. They didn't make a big deal about it, but they didn't lose sight of him as well, just in case he came up behind them with a gun.

Jerry went straight to the counter to ask for information on Officer Ramirez. The gentleman stated it was against their policy to state he lived in the complex. When Jerry showed him his badge, the guy agreed to help out. He couldn't find any tenant with the name Jerry had just given him. As Jerry headed in Michael's direction, four men were coming out of the elevator. As they walked out, Officer Ramirez came out of another elevator alone. The four gentleman that came out waited by the guest area, pretending to read some magazines.

As Officer Ramirez approached Michael and Jerry, he commented, "Gentlemen, the chief left me a message, something about having to go with you guys over some closed case. What exactly was he talking about? The last case I had was Captain Ross. Did new information come in? Was there something I missed?"

As he finished making his comments, Michael looked at him from head to toe. "Damn, Ramirez, what happened to you? You look like shit, man. Did someone run over you? Who beat the shit out of you?"

"Nobody, it's none of your business. I took care of that issue already myself?"

"Did you really take care of it? Did it have anything to do with you giving my personal information to El Checo? Did Pedro and his men have anything to do with your ass kicking? If so, I doubt you took care of it like you said."

As Michael finished making those comments, Ramirez's expression changed. Michael knew he had hit the jackpot. He knew they knew about him. Officer Ramirez stated he had to use the bathroom right after he would head out with them and correct any issue on that close case the chief was talking about.

As Ramirez walked into the restroom in the lobby, Michael and Jerry moved to a different location since they were giving their backs to those four men that had walked out of the elevator before Ramirez. As they positioned themselves to have a better look at all four men. One of them got a call, and as soon as he hung up, he made some signals to the other three. They all got up and pretended to leave the lobby.

As all four got up and started to walk out, all four of them pulled out their guns and all started shooting at us. Michael and Jerry quickly took cover. They shot back as much as they could, but their spots weren't that great of a hideout. As they responded on their second attempt, they noticed Ramirez running out of the restroom toward the four men shooting at them.

They looked around and found a way out the back. They didn't have the gun and manpower to match up to the four men. They were leaving the lobby when Michael noticed Pedro coming out of the elevators shooting at them as well. With all the shooting, all Michael heard from Pedro was, "Que no se escapen esos perros los quiero Muertos." (Don't let them escape, I want those dogs dead.)

Pedro didn't get his wish that day. Michael and Jerry were able to escape unharmed that time. Jerry called in the shooting and requested some backup. He asked Dispatch if anybody else had called in the shooting. Dispatch had stated no calls had been made about any shooting at that address. That automatically told them the personnel at this apartment complex was under Pedro's payroll as well.

Michael and Jerry ran a few blocks away from the shooting until they noticed they weren't following them anymore. As soon as they heard the sirens, Ramirez headed back to the apartment complex. As soon as Michael and Jerry got there, they noticed no dead bodies, just bullet holes all over the lobby. They called the chief to get them a warrant to get information on the tenants. It didn't take long. By the time an officer arrived with the warrant, they requested to speak to the manager and showed him the arrest warrant. And she followed to show them the list of all tenants.

They couldn't find any apartment under the name of Pedro or Officer Ramirez. If they were to go apartment after apartment, it was gonna be like looking for a needle in a haystack. They gave her all the paperwork she had given them. They thanked her for her time and left the area. They went straight to the office to discuss the situation with the chief. On their way to the office, Michael took out the backup phone he had purchased. He called Papa and wanted to see how everything had gone. Spoke to Casey as well; she was anxious. She couldn't wait to go hunting, and she asked him many times if he had gotten the missing items they were needing to go hunting.

"No, baby, I am still out doing that. I got busy at work, so I am barely heading that way. Will call you when I am done with all the purchasing." As soon as he hung up with her, he proceeded to call Sally. He wanted to see how she was doing. Based on what she told Michael, she was a bit shaken over an email she got. But she was doing a bit better than before.

Michael followed to let her know he was on his way to the office and would be busy throughout the day but would call her back as soon as he had a chance. As they hit the office, the chief questioned them on the spot.

"What exactly happened? All you were gonna do was pick up Ramirez and bring him in."

"Yes, Chief, that was the plan, but the suspicion we had about Ramirez has been confirmed. He is working with the Reynosa cartel. When we arrived, he was getting off the elevator. Four other men were getting off from a different one as well. But they headed to the lobby.

As Ramirez was about to leave with us, he gave us the restroom excuse. As he walked in, the four men sitting at the lobby surprised us with bullets coming left and right. Throughout the shooting back and forth, Ramirez came out running from the restroom in the direction of the four men. Soon after that, Pedro came out of the elevator shooting at us as well. If we ain't mistaken, it was five shooters, Pedro and Ramirez against us. And talking about Ramirez, Chief, he wasn't sick. He got his ass kicked, and real bad. I am assuming it was because him and Pedro weren't able to kill me that day at the restaurant. One of the persons I killed in self-defense turned out to be the son of El Checo, Reynosa drug cartel leader."

"Can you confirm this, Michael."

"Well, not yet, boss, but that's what Ramirez told us that day he was doing the report."

Michael gave Jerry a face signal as if trying to say, *Don't say any more.* Michael didn't want anybody else to know about the call he had gotten from El Checo earlier that day.

"Well, this is what I am gonna do," said the chief. "I am gonna order a twenty-four-hour surveillance on Ramirez's home. "He is bound to come home sooner or later. I will order a second surveillance on his wife. Just in case he orders her to meet him somewhere. That should be enough to get to him sooner or later."

"Chief, did you get any information on the video tapes on the day the drugs were stolen?"

"No, Michael, some way or another, those tapes got lost. We can't find them anywhere. We looked and looked, but they are nowhere to be found."

"That could have showed us who the second officer on Pedro's payroll is. Guess we are just gonna have to wait till he makes a mistake down the road."

As Michael made his last comment, the chief got a call and instructed them to leave. As they stepped out of the office, Michael asked Jerry who he had to ask to get my new vehicle.

"That's good that you remembered. Follow me, so you can fill out all the paperwork and take your new vehicle today." As Michael finished with all the paperwork, they headed out to pick up his new vehicle. Michael looked at Jerry and apologized to him.

"You know, Jerry, getting you involved in all this wasn't my intention. With you involved, there's a possibility they might go after you and your family as well."

"Don't worry, Michael, that's what partners are for, I will be by your side. And don't worry, I was thinking the same. I was already thinking of sending my family to the in-laws till we resolve this case. Till then, I am with you till the end, my friend."

Michael shook his hand and gave him a big tight hug. "It feels good to count on friends like you in moments like this. I will owe you one, remember that."

As they finished their chat, Michael got into his vehicle and headed to Dick's Sports Store. He went ahead and got some items they needed. As he finished, he headed up to the cabin to meet up with his parents and Casey.

CHAPTER 18

El Checo Starts His Payback

ICHAEL WAS HEADING HOME TO his parents' cabin, and as he got on the expressway, he got a call from Sally. I was waiting for your call, did you get busy?"

"Yes, I did. Was running errands back and forth, and honestly, I had totally forgotten I had told you I was gonna call you back. How are you feeling?"

"A bit better, I could say. The kids keep asking, why did I bring them to my parents' home? I had to tell them the house was gonna get remodeled and we couldn't stay in it while they worked on it."

"I am heading over to pick up some items I forgot to pack. I was curious if you wanted to meet me there if you like the idea."

Michael didn't think about it twice and responded, "As soon as you text me your address, I should be heading that way. Would really like to see you tonight."

"OK, let me text you the address and head that way. See you there."

After she hung up, Michael called his Papa to let him know he was gonna be a bit late. As he hung up on his call with his Papa, he got the message from Sally. He looked at the address and had an idea of where to go. On his way over there, he did a quick stop at a convenience store and bought some beer to relax the moment a bit more.

When he arrived, Sally was already waiting for him. He got out, got the beer, and headed to Sally's porch. Sally just smiled and made a comment: "You read my mind."

They both greeted each other with a big hug and a kiss right after they sat down on a wooden swing Sally had on her porch. Michael opened two beers—one for him and the other for Sally. They chatted the night away while they both drank some beer. Sally told him how dating a police officer had totally changed her life. She did state she meant it in a good way, not to take it as offensive. Michael gave her a kiss and commented, "If you ever feel this world is too much for you, by all means, let me know. Honestly, I will understand your point of view."

"I will," replied Sally. "When the time comes, I will let you know if something is bothering me. You know, Michael, when we had our first date, you didn't tell me your side of your story. You gave me the runaround. Why did you do that?"

"Because I didn't feel it was the correct time to let you know what had happened with my previous marriage."

If you cheated on her, I am telling you right now, this ain't gonna work, either."

"Stop talking nonsense. I didn't cheat on her. The reason she decided to walk out or end our marriage was because she was tired of being an officer's wife. After we got married, a few months later, I joined the undercover division. Every case was different. I was away from home for months, at times a whole year. She stated she was tired of waking up in fear of receiving that phone call letting her know I was killed in the line of duty.

"Oh wow, I definitely understand her point of view. But I see your mom, and she did great. I guess every woman is different. I ain't gonna guarantee you that I will stick through thick and thin. When it comes to those kind of cases. I ain't used to that life, yet this last dinner we had still has me shaking a bit. What I can promise you is that I will try my best day in and day out."

"That's good enough for me." And he followed to kiss her over and over again. The situation got a bit romantic because after all those hugs and kisses, Sally grabbed Michael's hand and led him to her room. They both must have been exhausted after their romantic night, because it was past 9:00 a.m. the next day, and both were still asleep. It was past 10:00 a.m. when Michael's phone started ringing. It took him a while, but when he found it, he followed to answer the call.

"Hello, James, did you forget our last conversation, cabron? I clearly told you if you would get the cops involved, I would get your family and their family involved as well."

"What the—"

"Shh," replied Checo, "when I am speaking, you shut up. I ain't done yet. I want you to stay close to your phone. Expect a phone call within the next two hours or so."

Michael was about to respond, but by then, Checo had already hung up on him. As he was replaying everything Checo had just said, he quickly called Stephanie. She didn't answer, so he went ahead and left her a voice mail. He quickly got up, took a shower, kissed Sally and told her he had to go. She tried to ask what was wrong, but Michael was out the door. She got her phone and sent him a message. As he got in his vehicle, he read the message, and he just replied, "Will explain later."

He drove to Stephanie's home, and when he arrived, he noticed a vehicle parked in the driveway. He got his gun out and carefully approached the vehicle. Nobody was inside, and as he looked up, he noticed the front door was wide open. He circled the house once; he didn't see anything out of the ordinary in the backyard. He slowly approached the front door and noticed it had a 12-gauge shot in the center of the door. As he walked in, he noticed the body of a dead man. It looked as though he had been brutally tortured before they killed him. The house was a total mess. He looked around and saw there was no trace of Stephanie anywhere in the house.

He crouched to the floor, dropped his gun, and placed both hands on each side of his face. Tears rolled down his face at the same time he screamed at Checo. "You better not touch her, you motherfucker. I will not stop till I kill you if you harm her in any way, shape, or form."

He stayed there crying his lungs out for a moment, when out of the blue, Jerry showed up out of nowhere.

"Are you OK?" asked Jerry as he stood by the door.

Michael wasn't expecting him. He reached for his gun when he heard his voice.

"Hey, hey, hold on, it's me, Jerry. Don't shoot."

"How did you know I was here?" asked Michael.

"I don't know, man. After yesterday's shooting, I went home with a bad feeling. I remembered you had said whoever would help you would be in trouble. I helped my wife and kids pack up and sent them away. I couldn't sleep all last night. I woke up super early. I called you several times, and you didn't answer. I thought the worse had happened to you already. I called the office and had your vehicle tracked, and here I am."

"Thanks for showing up. As you can see, Checo has started his payback. He took Stephanie sometime last night."

"How do you know it was last night and not this morning?"

"If I ain't that mistaken, this dead guy should be the man Stephanie was dating, and that vehicle out in the street should be his. Because Stephanie's vehicle is in the garage. And that vehicle out in the street has a cold motor already. Can you call it in, please. I need to know what time it happened."

"Why is that important?"

"Because if it wasn't that long, that means she is still here somewhere in Miami. If not, it means they took her to Mexico."

"I get you. Let me make the call. Be back in a bit."

Michael got up and headed up to Stephanie's room. As he walked in, he noticed the same two old English letters he had seen on the newspaper a few weeks ago. An old English SA. When he saw those two letters, he punched the wall as he walked downstairs. He met up with Jerry.

Michael told him, "It was that motherfucker. He left his mark up in the room. Did you call it in already?"

"Yes, I did," said Jerry.

"Make sure you let them know to do this on the down low. I don't want to see this on tomorrow's front page. They will put this killing and the one they had a few weeks ago together. They will notice it has the same initials."

"I will try my best, Michael. Won't promise you anything."

As he said that, Michael's phone started ringing. It was the chief. "Michael, just heard about the shootout. Ain't that your ex-wife's place?"

"Yes, sir, it is."

"Is she OK?" asked the chief.

"I don't know, Chief. She's nowhere to be found. All we got is a dead body lying in the living room. They didn't leave a note or anything. All they left were those two English letters they left at their last shootout. Chief, can I ask you for a big favor?"

"Of course you can, Michael. What can I do for you?"

"Can we keep the press out of this one please?"

"Sure we can, Michael, don't worry. Are you gonna need some help?"

"No, Chief, I am alone on this one. He already made it clear the more people I get involve, the more he will kill."

"Well then, I will instruct Jerry not to leave your side."

"No, Chief, it's OK. I got this."

"Well, after yesterday's shootout, looks like you probably don't have an option."

"Yeah, you might have a point. So only Jerry, and that's it, Chief."

"Sounds good. I will have a chat with Jerry."

"Chief, one last thing. Did you ever get those autopsy reports back on the captain and his wife?"

"As a matter of fact, Michael, now that you're mentioning it, I hadn't looked in to it. Been super busy day after day."

"Don't worry, Chief, I understand. Just keep me posted."

"Sure will, Michael. If you don't mind, Chief, once we can ID the victim, I would like to be the one to tell his family of what happened."

"Are you sure that's what you want, Michael?"

"Yes, Chief, I am sure."

"OK, if that's what you want, it's OK with me." As Michael hung up, Jerry just looked at him.

"What are your intentions?"

"My intention with what?" asked Michael.

"Well, you want to be the one to tell his family about his death."

"Come on, man, he was dating your ex-wife."

"I ain't seeing it like that, Jerry. Once I go tell them what happened, I plan to ask them for permission to search his home or apartment. You never know, I might find some clues at his place. Something that might help me find Stephanie. It doesn't hurt to give it a try."

"Yeah, I know what you mean. Once forensic and the investigators get here, if you don't mind, I would like to go with you."

"You know what, they say four eyes are always better than one. What I don't understand is with these gunshots on the door and walls, how is it that nobody reported the shooting when it happened?"

"Well, that might be something we can do when the officers arrived. We can go around the neighborhood and ask questions. Maybe then we can have the answers you seek, Michael."

"That would be a start."

When the officers arrived, Michael and Jerry headed out to the homes around Stephanie's home. They both asked each person that responded to their knocks. Some said they saw too many vehicles full of armed men. They didn't want any problems. Others said they saw some police vehicles involved. They assumed officers were aware. That's the reason no reports were done.

Michael had also asked around what time the shooting had occurred. They had all said around 4:00 a.m. So if Michael got his call around 10:00 a.m., that gave him only six hours. That wasn't enough time to reach Texas.

"She might still be in Miami, Jerry. We just need to follow the tips they left behind. I don't believe they are better than us. They might have a whole lot of guns and more man power than us, but that won't stop me, Jerry."

"I am right behind you, Michael, all the way. Just lead the way, and like you said, let's follow their tracks. That will lead us to Stephanie."

As they headed back to Stephanie's home, the officers were able to get more information on the dead body they had lying in the living room. As soon as they called in his first and last name, Dispatch returned right back with his DOB and address. They were able to confirm the address Dispatch had was the same one he had on his ID.

Jerry called in to the office. He wanted an officer to get more information on the dead body. They wanted to make sure his family was aware of what had just happened. Jerry signed away the wallet and keys that belonged to the dead body. He informed the investigator in charge that he would return them as soon as he was done with them. Michael and Jerry left the home and headed to the dead body's home. All the way, Michael just stared at the identification. All he knew at this point was that his name was Tracy Greene. He had been the one Stephanie had been talking about the other day. She had stated she had a wonderful dinner date. When they arrived at his address, they were to tell the guy had money. He had a lovely home. They parked outside and decided to walk in and take a look to see what they could find. Once they were inside, they were able to determine that Tracy Greene was the owner of a nice jewelry store in downtown Miami. When they reached his room, they noticed he had left his laptop on and what appeared to be instructions on how to activate a tracking device on a charm bracelet or some type of jewelry. Based on the price tag he left behind, it was expensive.

Michael didn't know if the tracking device was for insurance purposes or he was the jealous type. Jerry told Michael of a good computer geek he knew. Maybe he could be of some help. Michael tried to mess with the laptop but had no luck.

"That guy you're talking about could be of some help after all, Jerry."

They gathered everything Tracy had left behind on the bed and headed over to meet up with the geek friend Jerry had mentioned. Once they reached the location, Michael asked Jerry to gather the information needed. He told him he had to call his dad and see how Casey was doing. His father told him everybody was doing great, just that Casey was a bit anxious to know when the hunting trip was gonna start.

Michael followed to tell his father what had happened with Stephanie. He told his father not to tell Casey anything, but he would keep his father informed. He asked if she was still alive.

"I don't know. All I know is she was kidnapped. Don't have an idea where she might be."

"Be careful, Michael, that's all I ask from you."

"I will, Papa. I will. If anything happens at the cabin, please let me know."

"We will be OK, Michael. Don't worry about us." When he finished talking with his father, Jerry walked out.

"We are good to go. I got great news, Michael."

"Great news? What are you talking about, Jerry?"

"I told you this guy was good. Get in the car. You drive while I explain everything to you. This guy was able to unblock the laptop. You were correct, Michael. He did activate a tracking device on a piece of jewelry. We don't know if he gave it to Stephanie or not, but the laptop is tracking something down at 14331 SW 139 ct. Let's head that way and see what we will find."

CHAPTER 19

On His Way to Find Stephanie

ERRY AND MICHAEL WERE ON their way to see what the laptop was tracking when all of a sudden, Michael got a video text message. He pulled over to see who it was from. It came from Checo. As he opened it, Checo appeared in the video first.

"Remember me, James Summers? Or should I say Michael Brown. I told you very clearly this was between me and you. Not to get anybody else involved, or I would take it out on your family and the other person's family helping you out as well. I will take that as a yes. Let me know if you know who this person is." The phone was pointed to Stephanie. She had signs of torture and a few bruises on her face. She was wearing a blindfold with gray duct tape covering her mouth.

Checo continued to comment, "And this is just the beginning, Michael. Don't forget you started this, we didn't." And the video text was over.

Michael tried so much to be strong, but he couldn't. He broke down in tears. Banging the steering wheel over and over again. Jerry got off and told him to hit the passenger side. He would continue the drive while he controlled himself. Jerry was out of words. He didn't have a clue what to say. He had been in this situation before, but the people he had to talk to was people he didn't know. It was part of his job to say those words to make them feel better and give them a bit more hope. Always telling them their significant other would be found.

This time it was his friend, his partner. Jerry grabbed his shoulder, and all he could say was, "We will get him, Michael. He will pay for this. I guarantee you that I won't leave your side till we get him, if it means going to the end of the world, but we will find him." Michael wiped his tears and thanked him.

He regained control of himself and continued to give Jerry direction of where to go. Once they got to the place, they parked a few blocks away. They continued on their way on foot. The area they were at was mainly all warehouses, all being used for shipping and receiving. Most of them had big semi trucks being loaded, and some were being unloaded. When they reached the warehouse they were getting the signal from, they approached it with caution. They didn't see any SUV or cop cars as the people at Stephanie's neighborhood had stated they had seen.

They entered the warehouse by one of the side doors. The strange thing was it wasn't locked. They felt as though they were waiting for them. As soon as they both entered the place, they were both received with gunshots. Jerry and Michael quickly took cover. Jerry was able to count seven men in total. The gunshots went back and forth for a while. Jerry and Michael were running out of ammo, and they still had four men left.

Michael instructed Jerry to head over to the vehicle. He told him he had some ammo in the trunk. Jerry quickly left to retrieve the ammo while Michael wisely used up the little ammo he had left. By the time Jerry was back Michael had already gotten one more, leaving just three men still shooting at them. By the time they had taken all the men out, someone had already reported the shooting.

Four uniformed cops arrived at the warehouse. Michael and Jerry showed them their badges and told them everything was under control. They ordered them to surround the warehouse and look for any suspicious men fleeing the area. As the cops left to look around, Michael and Jerry made sure all seven men were dead. As they checked all the men, Michael was able to identify one of them. The guy in charge just happened to be El Pilas, one of Pedro's gunmen. He told Jerry he had met him while being undercover.

They continued to look around the warehouse. They were still trying to find out what was it that led them to the warehouse. As Jerry reached the office, he found some clothes on the ground. They were soaked with blood. He called Michael over to take a look at what he had found. When Michael reached the office, he was able to determine it was the same clothes Stephanie was wearing on the video.

As he went through them, he noticed a bracelet on the ground. He looked at Jerry. Could this be it. "Is this the item we were tracking? It looks expensive to me," said Jerry.

"Did you find anything else?" Michael asked Jerry.

"No, the whole warehouse is empty. This could mean two things. These guys were waiting for us. Or Checo and Pedro just left with Stephanie. Because the warehouse was still open, it wasn't locked."

As they headed out the warehouse, more officers arrived. Jerry told them the warehouse was clear. He told them to bag the clothes and the bracelet that was in the office. He told them to match the blood with the blood they found at Stephanie's home. Just to confirm, it was Stephanie's clothes that was left behind."

Michael signaled Jerry that wasn't necessary. He knew for a fact they did belong to her. As they both walked back to Michael's vehicle, Jerry got a call. "Officer Sanders, yes, how can I help you?"

"Sir, I am Officer Thompson. I am the lead officer doing the surveillance on Officer Ramirez wife. The purpose of my call is to inform you she has entered the grocery store. About five minutes ago, Officer Ramirez arrived as well. I tried calling the chief, but he didn't answer. He gave me this number as a second number to report any activity."

"Forward me the address as soon as possible. If Officer Ramirez leaves, follow him and not his wife, understood?"

As he hung up, Jerry gave Michael the great news. Jerry took passenger, and Michael drove away. When he got the address, he quickly instructed Michael where to go. When they arrived, Officer Ramirez was still with his wife at the grocery store. Jerry instructed the officers that they would take over from there and had them follow the wife as soon as she came out.

They were outside waiting. Thirty minutes had passed already, and they had no sign of either one. Jerry called Officer Thompson an instructed him to head inside the grocery store to make sure they were still in the store. After the officer reached the store, a few minutes later, Officer Ramirez and his wife were walking out.

Ramirez got in a totally different car. Guess he had ditched his patrol car. Michael and Jerry followed him a few cars behind. Ramirez didn't even notice he was being followed. He drove over to Chase Bank, parked his car, and walked in to the bank.

"Are you thinking what I am thinking?" said Jerry. "Well, if you were thinking of a way to get in his car, and surprise him while he drove away guess we were."

"No, Michael, I got a feeling he is planning his getaway. He has no way out. What we know about him, sooner or later, we will arrest him. Once we do, he will spend the rest of his days in jail. That meeting at the grocery store was to have his wife to get her stuff ready. He came here to get all his money out. He is planning his getaway—that's what he is doing."

"You might be right, Jerry. What we need to do is find a way to get close to him without him noticing us. Let me check if his doors are locked. Will be back in a bit."

As Michael approached the car, he checked all the doors, and they were all locked. His second option was to puncture one of his tires. As he was doing so a Chase security guard approached Michael and questioned him. He stated that he was gonna be detained for vandalism.

Michael showed him his badge and instructed them not to interfere in their investigation. As the security guard left the area, Michael headed back to the car.

"What was all that about?" asked Jerry.

"Well, all his doors are locked. We need a plan B. I had no option but to puncture one of his tires. That will give us time to approach him as he changes the tire. But as I was doing that, the security guard wanted to detain me. I showed him my badge, and that was it."

Jerry and Michael waited and waited. It took Ramirez a total of thirty minutes. By the time he came out of the bank, they noticed he came out with a briefcase. As Ramirez approached the vehicle, he noticed his flat tire. As he started to change the tire, Michael and Jerry approached him quietly. He didn't even notice them. By the time he realized they were behind him, he attempted to get his gun out. Jerry got his shoulder and made him a sign with his hand, like telling him, *Don't try it, mister.*

Michael took the gun away from him and got the briefcase as well. They ordered him to head over to their vehicle. Ramirez and Jerry got in the back seat while Michael got in the driver's seat. He asked Ramirez for the password to the briefcase, but he refused to give it to him.

Jerry didn't think about it twice and hit him right on his face with the grip of the gun. It must have been hard because he busted Ramirez's nose, followed by a big gush of blood. As Jerry attempted to strike him again, Ramirez made him a sign, like trying to say he had had enough. He didn't think about it twice this time. The one blow to his face had caused him some damage. He gave them the password.

As Michael opened the briefcase, his face changed completely. "Wow, look at this, Jerry. How much would you think is in here?"

Jerry took a peek. "I would say enough for our retirement, don't you think."

Ramirez yelled out, "Keep it all. Just let me go. I won't say a word about the money. It's yours to keep."

Michael closed the briefcase and just laughed at Ramirez. "What makes you think we were gonna let you keep it?" Michael got his gun out and cocked it and pointed it at Ramirez's face.

"You know very well what I want. You know what you did last night. Give me the exact location of where they took her."

"All I know is they took her to some warehouse."

"She ain't there. We found the warehouse already. All we found was Stephanie's belongings."

"Well, I don't know where they took her. That's the last place I knew about."

"Bullshit," Michael replied. "How much is your life worth, Ramirez?"

"I am being serious, Brown," Ramirez cried out.

Right after Ramirez finished making his comment, Michael fired a round, but shot him in the leg. "Tell me where they took her, or next one is going in your forehead."

While Ramirez grabbed his leg, he continued to tell Michael he didn't know. "After we took her from her house last night, I followed them to the warehouse. At that point, I realized I didn't want to be involved. That's the reason I met with my wife. We were supposed to leave the country. She was gonna head home, pack some bags, and I was gonna get this money out. That's all I know."

"Has Pedro or Checo called you lately?"

"I don't report to Checo. I report to Pedro, and no, he hasn't called me since I left the warehouse this morning. Tell you what, I know some hideouts Pedro has. You will go with us said Michael Meanwhile, take your belt off, cut your shirt, do something to your wound so you won't bleed out on us. Because I sure ain't taking you to a hospital just yet. And give me your phone just in case Pedro calls you and you have your phone on silent."

As Michael drove to one of the few locations he got to visit, Ramirez's phone rang. Michael wasn't able to tell if it was Pedro. The caller ID showed an anonymous caller. Michael pulled over and gave the phone to Ramirez.

"Answer the call and put it on speaker. We want to hear everything."

As Ramirez answered the call, Pedro asked him, "Where you at?"

"Just leaving the grocery store. Just met up with my wife."

"Is anybody following you?"

"Not that I know of. Why, what's going on?"

"Checo wants you to get some information on that officer helping Michael out. We are going after his family next. Checo made it clear to Michael he would go after anybody that would help him out. Once you get that information, head over to our last meeting point. I will be waiting for you there."

"Sounds good. Just give me some time."

"Don't take long," replied Pedro and then hung up.

"So he wants to come after my family. He don't know what he has coming his way," said Jerry. "So you heard him, where did you all meet up last? We want that address." Jerry pointed his gun to Ramirez's head. "Michael missed the head shot. Believe me, I ain't."

"Ok, OK, the last time we met up, it was over in North Miami. It was down 125th Street corner of 9th and 124th."

"Did you get that, Michael?"

"I sure did." Michael quickly turned the car around and headed that way. When they arrived, they noticed three SUVs parked on the side of the road. No one seemed to be guarding the home. They could see smoke coming from the backyard. It seemed as though they were having some barbecue because they had some live music playing as well.

"Looks like these guys are celebrating Stephanie's kidnapping. Do they honestly feel they have won this battle?" Michael parked a few blocks away.

"What do you have in mind, Michael?" replied Jerry.

"Let's get our guns and some extra ammo ready. I don't want the same situation we had at the warehouse to happen again. This time I am gonna get prepared. If Stephanie is in that house, I am coming out with her."

"Let me help you."

"No, you keep that gun pointed at that scumbag. I don't want him to warn them we are about to arrive." As soon as Michael had everything ready, he asked Jerry to get Ramirez out.

"Let's go, sucker. You're gonna be our shield, just in case we turn out to be the surprised ones."

Michael had Ramirez call Pedro to let him know he had arrived . Pedro informed him the door was open, and he was heading upstairs. He told Ramirez the guys were out in the back, and he would be down in a bit.

Michael signaled Jerry. He wanted Jerry to go after the men, and he would go after Pedro. Jerry agreed. By the time he hit the backyard and the first three rounds was fired, Michael was already halfway up the stairs. Jerry still had Ramirez as his shield as he took the first three shots. He was able to get three of them. The other four that were there shot some rounds at him but didn't hit him. Each bullet fired hit Ramirez, killing him on the spot.

By then, Pedro was running out from one of the rooms on the second floor. By the time he ran out of the room, Michael was already waiting for him. He shot some rounds at him but didn't get him. Pedro fired back on the spot.

"If you came this far, Michael, let me guess, Checo sent you the video already."

"Yes, and I am here to take her with me," replied Michael.

"She ain't here, man. Checo took her to Mexico already."

"Bullshit. You know you're hiding her in one of these rooms."

Some more rounds were shot between each other.

"She ain't here, cabron. What part don't you understand? I will make you a deal. If your cojones are as big as mine, let's take care of this like two men. No guns."

"I know that trick already, Pedro. I won't fall for that."

As soon as Michael made that comment, two guns were thrown to the hallway from the room where Pedro was at.

"Those are the only guns I got. Put yours down, y vengase, cabron." (Come at me, sucker.)

Michael put his gun down and walked into the room were Pedro was at. He was already in his fighting stance, waiting for him .

"Vengase, cabron, vamos a ver quien es más chingon de los dos." (Let's go, sucker. Let's find out who is tougher out of the two of us).

As Michael and Pedro initiated their fight, Jerry was still downstairs shooting away with the few men he still had to eliminate. He wasn't hearing any shots being fired from Michael's direction. That got him worried. He thought the worst had happened. He had assumed Pedro and Michael had killed themselves. He fought his way out of the backyard and then headed upstairs, looking for Michael. His whole way up the stairs, he continued to shoot his way up. He arrived at the room where Pedro and Michael were at. That distracted Michael, and that helped Pedro to get Michael in a chokehold and point a knife to his neck.

"Drop your gun, or he dies on the spot."

Jerry walked into the room, trying to get closer to them.

Pedro screamed again, "Get any closer, and he dies."

At the same time, Michael yelled out, "Just take your shot! What are your waiting for?" Right after Michael's comment, the remaining shooters approached the room. Pedro instructed them to put their guns down. He would take care of the issue himself.

As Pedro's men put their guns down, Jerry took his stand and aimed his gun at Pedro. "Are you sure you want to die today, my friend?"

"You might kill me with that one shot, but keep in mind, I still have four armed men waiting to unload their guns on you guys. Tell you what," said Pedro, "nobody has to die today. I owe my life to this fuckin' traitor. I am a man of my word. When he saved my life, I told him then if he ever needed anything, I would be the man to help him out. Your wife ain't here, Michael. Checo has taken her already, and you know where that location is at."

As he finished making those comments, he let Michael go. Consider yourself paid back for saving my life at that shootout. But I guarantee you, if we ever meet again, one of us will have to die. Now leave my place and don't look back, before I regret my decision and kill you both."

Michael picked up his gun and walked away slowly. He still was in shock that Pedro had let them go.

"What's this all about?" whispered Jerry to Michael.

"I will explain it to you later. Let's get the hell out of here first. Where is Ramirez?" asked Michael.

"He didn't make it," replied Jerry. I continued to use him as my shield as I killed three of the gunmen. They fired back, and they killed him."

"Well, then, don't worry about him and let's get out of here."

CHAPTER 20

On Their Way to Mexico

S THEY WERE LEAVING THE area, Jerry looked at Michael. "Can you explain to me now what exactly was that all about?"

Michael just smiled and responded. "Take it as our luckiest day in our lives."

"No, man, I am serious. Tell me what freaking drug dealer would let you go just like Pedro did. No freaking dealer would ever do that." I saved his life while I was undercover. He went in to charge some money they owed him. But it was all a setup. As he walked into the place, a few more men entered the building right behind him. All of them were fully loaded. As the shootout started, I had no choice. I was stuck in the middle of the case. This guy was gonna take me to meet Checo. I needed him alive, so I went in to help him out. So that's the reason he stated he owed me a favor."

"I get you now, so where are we going now? I am going to my place. I am gonna need my passport. Then I will head over to your place to drop you off."

"Drop me off? What the hell are you talking about, man? I told you very clearly I am with you till the end. You heard the man. They are going after my family next. So we need to make sure we get them first before they kidnap anybody else from our family. So with that being said, go get your passport and head to my place to go pick up mine as well."

"You do know it's a long drive to Mexico," said Jerry.

"Who said anything about driving? Ramirez left us his share. We are gonna fly down to Texas. Then drive down to Mexico."

"Michael, are you sure you know what you're doing? We are gonna go pick a fight on his turf. It's mentioned everywhere the cartels run the show down in Mexico, not the government."

"If I were to tell you I have an ace under my sleeve, would you believe me?"

"What other choice do I have?" replied Jerry. When they arrived at Jerry's place, Michael instructed him not to pack too many clothes, just enough for two days max. And if you have those tourist waist pouches, bring that as well. As Jerry got in the vehicle, Michael called his father to keep him informed and to ask how Casey was doing as well. As his Papa answered, Michael gave him a briefing of what was going on and what his plans were gonna be.

"Going down to Mexico is too risky, Michael. You know there's a possibility you might not come back at all. What will we tell Casey, then?

"We got to be positive about all this, Papa. I promise you I will be back. Give Casey a kiss from me, and see you guys in a few days." After he hung up, he called Sally see how she was doing . She was busy with the kids at the moment but did state she was worried about him. She hadn't heard anything from him throughout the whole day. Michael gave her minimum information. He did state he would be out of the country for a few days but would be back soon. He told Sally if she needed anything to call his father. He would help her out with anything she needed.

When he hung up, Jerry had already packed his items, and Michael was on his way home to pack his items. On their way to Michael's place, Jerry asked him, "So, Michael, what exactly is our plan gonna be? It's me and you against a whole army in a totally different country. We don't know what to expect. The plan is this, Jerry: Down in Reynosa, there is an officer that just happens to hate Pedro and their cartel," said Michael.

"And how exactly do you know this?" asked Jerry.

"Pedro brought took me their to meet Checo on our way to his place. The Mexican police had a checkpoint. There at that checkpoint was where I met him. He is my only hope. When we arrive in Mexico, we will look for him. After I tell him our situation, there's a chance he might want to help us out. If his answer is no, then, Jerry, as you said before, it's just you and me against a whole army. When they arrived at Michael's place, he quickly packed his items, and they headed to the airport.

"Jerry, quick question," said Michael. "Who do you bank with?"

"Bank of America, why you asking?"

"Great. So do I," said Michael. "This is what we are gonna do. We will stop at the bank, grab some money from Ramirez's bag, and each of us will deposit some money on our accounts. We will need that money when we arrive in Mexico. Did you bring that kangaroo waist bag I asked you for?"

"No," replied Jerry, "I didn't have one."

"Don't worry, they might have some at the airport."

"And what you want that for?" asked Jerry. "Well, I was thinking of stashing about 40k on each of our bags. That would give us 80k total, plus what we deposit at the bank. We are gonna need a vehicle, ammo, guns, you name it. All that will need to be purchased in México. I ain't gonna run the risk of crossing them and being caught.

"I get you now," replied Jerry. "Let's go and make the deposits."

After they each made the deposit, they headed to the airport. They quickly stopped by the souvenir shop and purchased the kangaroo waist pouches Michael had wanted. They hid the money there and continued on to purchase the plane tickets. As they went through security, they placed their bags on the conveyor belt. The officer instructed them to place the kangaroo waist pouches as well. Michael and Jerry just stared at each other and did as instructed.

They were cleared by the security officer; no alarms were activated. But their kangaroo waist pouches didn't have the same luck. Jerry and Michael were instructed to go to a secured room, where they would be questioned about their finding. When they both reached the room, they sat down and were told an officer would be in to question them. As they sat down, Jerry gave Michael a sign, like letting him know he had this.

When the officer arrived, he introduced himself and showed them the kangaroo pouches with the money exposed. "Do you care to explain what this is for, and why it wasn't declared to us?"

Jerry stood up and introduced himself. He got his badge out and showed it to the officer. "This is Officer Brown. We are working an undercover case."

Michael shook his hand as well and showed him his badge. "The information on the case is minimum. We cannot give you full details about it. All we can inform you is the case has gone south on us . We got a tip the person we are pursuing has headed down to Texas with intentions of crossing to Mexico. Our goal is to arrest him before he crosses to Mexico. Our department is aware of our actions, but we are trying to keep it on the down low. Don't want this kind of information to hit the news. You being an officer, I am sure you know what we mean by it."

"Sure, I definitely understand your point of view. Give me a minute. I will be taking your badges. Will make some calls just to make sure they are legit. I will be back in a bit."

"Sure, take your time. We have about an hour to spare" said Jerry.

When the officer came back, he gave Jerry his badge back and commented, "Gentlemen, seems we have a bit of a problem."

"What kind of a problem?" asked Jerry.

"Well, your information came back you work Homicide Division, is that correct?"

"That's correct," replied Jerry.

"But on Mr. Brown, we didn't get any information back."

As he made that comment, Michael got his phone out and gave him a number. "Call this number," he said. "I work undercover cases, my information won't come out just like Jerry's did. That number belongs to Chief White. He should be able to tell you any information you need on me and confirm that badge does belong to me.

"Let me make another call, be back in a bit," said the officer.

About ten minutes after he had walked out of the room, Jerry got a call from Chief White. When Jerry answered the call, the chief questioned him with a very strong voice, making it seem like he was bothered by the call he had just received.

"Jerry, can you please explain what the hell is going on? Why is an officer from Miami International Airport calling me to get information on Michael?"

"It's a long story, boss. All I can say is our clues are leading us to Texas."

"TEXAS!" Chief White yelled. "That is way out of our jurisdiction, Jerry, and you know that."

"Yes, sir, I do. The officer is back. Let me get with him. Will call you back in a bit, Chief."

When the airport officer came back, he was able to confirm Michael's identify. He returned his badge to him along with their kangaroo waist pouches and let them go. As they got out of the room, Michael asked Jerry, "What did the chief tell you?"

"Nothing good, Michael. He didn't sound too happy about our trip to Texas. I told him I would call him back, but what the hell, we are already halfway. Might as well go. We can deal with him later, what do you think."

"I don't have a choice, Jerry. Regardless of what he tells me, I need to get Stephanie back. Even if it means me losing my job," said Michael.

After spending some time in the investigation room, their wait for their flight wasn't that much anymore. It was past 9:00 p.m. by the time they arrived at McAllen Miller International Airport. They both agreed it would be too dangerous to cross to Mexico that late at night. They grabbed a taxi and headed to the nearest hotel. When they arrived at the hotel, they put their stuff away, took a quick shower, and planned out what they were gonna do the next day.

As Michael was lying down staring at the ceiling, he got a message on his phone. He opened it and noticed it was from Checo. The message said, "Looks like you turned out to be a smart cop. But a dumb one as well. What makes you think you will get to me on my own territory?"

As he closed his phone, he looked at Jerry. "It ain't gonna be easy, Jerry. He knows we are coming after him. Pedro must have warned him already."

"What did he text you?" asked Jerry.

"What makes us think we will get to him on his own turf?"

"He has a point, Michael."

"Let's just hope that Mexican officer decides to help us out. With his help, it will be a whole lot easier for both of us. Let's rest and figure that out tomorrow," said Michael. It was 7:00 a.m. by the time Jerry and Michael checked out of their hotel. They grabbed a taxi and asked him to take them to Reynosa.

The driver said the closest he could take them would be Hidalgo, Texas. His company didn't allow him to cross to Mexico. Michael asked how far Hidalgo was from Reynosa. The driver stated he would drop them off at the crossing point. They both agreed and headed to Hidalgo. When they reached their destination, the taxi driver gave them instruction of where to go. They paid him and headed their way. As they crossed the border, they quickly got a taxi and asked him to take them to their local police station. When they arrived, Michael asked to speak to Officer Romero. The person that assisted him asked what the issue was about. If possible, he would be able to assist them .

Michael insisted he wanted to speak to Officer Romero. The issue he had could be resolved only by him. The person that assisted him informed Michael the Officer Romero he knew was a federal officer, not a local officer. It was gonna be hard to locate him.

Michael asked what the difference was between a federal and a local officer. The gentleman assisting him continued to explain to him that a local officer patrolled only the city or area he was assigned to. A federal officer patrolled the whole state of Tamaulipas. There was a slim chance Officer Romero was out of town. It didn't hurt to give it a try.

"Give me a minute. Will be back with you guys in a bit. After he left his desk, Jerry looked at Michael.

"Is his position just like a state trooper?"

"Don't have a clue," said Michael. His position must be higher than that. His father-in-law is the governor of this state. I don't think the man would have his son-in-law as a patrol officer."

When the officer came back, he approached Michael. "Looks like you guys are in luck. I was able to locate Officer Romero. He stated he would arrive to assist you guys in about an hour or so. Would you guys care to wait or come back in an hour?"

"Well, we haven't had breakfast yet. We will be heading to a close-by restaurant and be back in a bit. Can you let him know Michael Brown will be back in about an hour? Let him know it's important I speak to him."

"Sure will," replied the officer at the counter. "I will let him know when he arrives."

"Do you know of a good restaurant we can stop by and have breakfast?" asked Jerry.

"I sure do. As soon as you exit the building, take a right two blocks down. It's called Gorditas Doña Tota."

"Thanks. We will be back in an hour."

They left the building and headed out as the officer had stated. They were able to find the place but were having an issue ordering what they wanted to eat. For one, the menu was in Spanish, and the person taking the orders didn't speak English. The good thing was the place was a bit packed. Jerry and Michael pointed at what they thought looked good and told the person what they wanted. When they got their orders, they took their first bite, and both really loved what they had gotten. After they finished their meal, they asked the person at the counter to serve them another round of what he had given them. As they were enjoying their second orders, Officer Romero showed up and sat with them.

"Good morning, gentlemen. I am Officer Romero, nice to meet you. I got a message that you guys requested to speak to me. How can I help you?"

Jerry introduced himself as Michael was about to do the same. Officer Romero stared at him. "You look familiar. Have we met before?"

"Actually, we have," replied Michael. "That is what brought us here to Reynosa,and the reason we came looking for you. I am Officer Michael Brown, and this is Officer Jerry Sanders. We both work for Miami Dade PD."

"Miami police officers," Romero replied with a smile. "What has brought you guys to my hometown? Hope you guys ain't flashing your badges around here. If so, let me tell you guys I can arrest you on the spot."

"No, sir, it ain't like that," replied Michael. "Do you have time, because the story will be a bit long."

"Well, it depends. I do have some issues to attend . If your story does not pertain to me, I'll let you know any other officer can assist you. If the story interests me, believe me, you will have my undivided attention."

"Well, the story is like this: I was working an undercover case up in Miami. The case was to arrest a local drug dealer by the name of Pedro Salinas."

"Pedro Salinas, the same guy associated with the Reynosa cartel," replied Romero.

"Yes, that same guy, but then we didn't know he was associated with the cartel. As I worked on the case, Pedro brought me here to meet up with his boss, El Checo."

"That's right," responded Romero. "You're that gringo that was in the vehicle a few weeks ago when you all drove through that checkpoint."

"Yes, that was me," replied Michael.

"So what do you guys need from me?" asked Romero.

"Well, the case didn't go as we had planned. We were able to confiscate the drugs, but Pedro got away. It turned out they had some officers working in their payroll. Thanks to them, we assume they got their drugs back but murdered the captain in charge of the case. A few days after that, I was out having dinner with my family. El Checo's boy was in the area causing some trouble with his bodyguards. They killed some people. I was in the area and ended up killing him. El Checo got ahold of all my information and found out I was the same person he had at his place while working undercover. He has made it clear that he will take all my family down one by one till I suffer as much as he is suffering for the death of his child. My ex-wife was kidnapped by him, and he is holding her at his place here in Reynosa. That's the reason we are here. Based on the information Pedro gave me that day you pulled us over, he sure made it sound like you were one of his worst rivals. That's the reason why I am here. We need your help getting my ex-wife back."

"I will be honest, hitting the Reynosa cartel has been my dream. But that ain't something I can do just right off the bat. Let me make some calls, speak to my father-in-law. If what you're saying is correct, I can use that to my advantage and get something going. For now I will have my men take you to a safe place. You too will stay there till I come pick you up. By all means, do not attempt to play that hero role you guys are used to up in Miami. If something is gonna happen, I will be the one to lead the way," said Romero.

"Sounds good," replied Jerry and Michael. They both got in a vehicle Romero pointed to and headed to a hotel.

CHAPTER 21

Waiting for Romero's Response

IT WAS PAST 10:00 A.M., and Romero hadn't showed up yet. Michael was anxious; he couldn't wait any longer. He got up from his bed and told Jerry he would be back.

"Hey, hold on there. Mr. Romero wanted us to wait here. He clearly said not to move or step out of the hotel."

"Jerry, neither your ex-wife or Romero's ex-wife ain't the one being hold captive. For what I know, he probably killed her already. If Romero ain't gonna help us, I need to do something about it, and I need to do it now."

"I understand your pain, Michael, but you need to understand we don't live here. We don't know our way around here. Just like we could be robbed, they can also kill us. We don't even have guns to protect ourselves. Just be patient, that's all I am asking you. Keep in mind and think about what you're asking from him. You're asking him to help us attack a drug cartel. That same cartel you yourself mentioned controls this place. So it ain't as easy as you think to just get up, gather some men, and go out and start a war."

Michael opened the door, looked at Jerry. "You have a point. But so do I. I will be downstairs. I will only wait one more hour. If he doesn't show up, I will step out and see what I can do on my own. I remember Pedro stated the cartel has some enemies here in town. They were supposed to supply me with forty kilos of cocaine . But their local stash houses got raided by their enemies here in Reynosa."

"Just be careful, Michael, that's all I am asking you. If he happens to show up and you ain't here, let's get our story straight right now. You stepped out to get something to eat, are we clear on that?"

"That will work," replied Michael. He went downstairs and stepped outside the hotel. As he was standing outside, a child carrying a shoeshine box stood in front of him.

"Shoeshine, mister. Two dollars," said the child.

"Sure," said Michael, "why not."

The child happily got comfortable and started shining Michael's shoes. The boy's English wasn't that great, but living out on the streets, he was able to pick up a few words here and there.

"You from Texas, mister?" asked the boy, trying to make conversation while he shined Michaels shoes.

"No, I ain't," said Michael. I am from Florida."

"Oh, next to Texas," replied the boy.

Michael just smiled. "Yeah, about twenty-four hours from Texas. I am Michael, what's your name?"

"Name?" the boy replied.

"Yeah." Michael tapped his chest and said, "I am Michael. How about you?"

"Oh, mi nombre, name, oh, OK, I am Oscar, mucho gusto." (A pleasure to meet you.)

"Same here," said Michael.

As the child was about to start shining the second shoe, Romero arrived. "Will be waiting for you upstairs," he said.

Michael paid the boy, told him one shoe was OK, and followed Romero. As they both entered the room, Michael didn't like the face Romero had when he came in. "You look like you don't have good news for us," he said.

"Honestly, guero, I don't, as much as I want to help you out. I got strict orders from my father-in-law not to attack."

"Did he give you a reason?" asked Jerry.

"No, he didn't," said Romero.

Michael pulled out his phone and showed him the video text he had received from El Checo. This is the reason why I am here, and I won't leave this place till I find her. After seeing the video Romero said he wanted to help them with the attack, but he knew he couldn't go against his father-in-law's orders.

"Can I ask you something and you promise me to be honest with your response?" asked Michael.

"Sure, what's your question?" said Romero.

"What happens to people who mess with the cartel?"

"They kill them on the spot. We have plenty of unsolved murders for that same reason?"

"What do they do with the cops?"

"Where are you trying to go with your questions, guero?"

"Answer my questions," replied Michael.

"Well, the cops that agree to work with them get rich and live a happy life, until the cartel don't need them anymore and they end up dead years from now."

"How about the officers that refuse to work with them?" asked Michael.

"We find them dead as well."

"Now answer me this: How long have you been giving the cartel a hard time?"

"For years now," replied Romero.

"Why do you think they haven't killed you, because of your father-in-law. Keep that in mind" said Michael. "With the troubles you have given them, just think about it. You know for a fact that is enough reason to find you dead in a ditch at any moment."

"Be careful with what you say, guero. That happens to be my father-in-law, and the governor of Tamaulipas. A well-known, well-respected man, I should say."

"I am just trying to open your eyes, that's all, Romero."

"I can't do much, but I know a guy that can help you guys out. Based on the video you showed me, I know for a fact you're going to attack regardless of what I do or say."

"You got that right," replied Michael.

Romero got a piece of paper and wrote a name and number. "Call this man. He will be waiting for your phone call. If someone can do something for you guys other than me, it sure will be that man. And be careful, gringos, this ain't Miami, and you two ain't Miami Vice, cabrones." He turned around an left the room.

"Do you think he got your point when you told him the reason he is still alive?" asked Jerry.

"I hope so, Jerry. We need his help. Without him, we sure will be outnumbered."

"With gun power and manpower, amigo," yelled Jerry. "Let's give him some time so he can call this number he gave us. Let's hope this man can be of some help to us."

"I ain't waiting," said Michael. He got the paper and headed downstairs. He told the front desk he needed to make a call. He showed them the number, and they directed him to a booth. When Michael picked up the phone, a voice was already asking for Michael Brown.

"This is him, who am I speaking with?" asked Michael.

"That ain't important," said the voice on the other end. "Romero said you guys would need some help from me."

"Did he tell you our situation and what we need?"

"He didn't give me the whole picture, but he gave me enough to say you too pinche gringos are crazy. In an hour, a red four-door ford will be outside of the hotel waiting for you guys. Get in the truck, and they will bring you to me."

"Just like that, with no questions asked," said Michael.

"Who needs the help? I do or you do?" said the voice on the other end.

"OK, we will be here waiting, then," said Michael. He went back up to the room, got his stuff, and instructed Jerry to follow him.

"Where are we going?" asked Jerry .

Across the street to go get something to eat."

"And for that, we need to take all of our stuff?" asked Jerry.

"Just get your stuff, man. I will explain everything once we get to the restaurant."

On their way down to the hotel lobby, Michael was explaining to Jerry what had just happened. As they crossed the road, Jerry pointed out, "Michael, there's a red Ford coming this way already."

"It ain't that one. The guy said within an hour, and it's only been ten minutes."

When they arrived at the restaurant, they sat down and ordered some Cokes. As the waiter brought them their drinks, he also gave them the menus. "English or Spanish?" asked the waiter with an accent.

"English please," said Jerry.

"OK, let me know when you're ready to order. Be back in a minute," said the waiter.

As they both opened the menus, they both felt a big relief. On these ones, they at least had some pictures to go with the name of the plate they were offering. They weren't able to pronounce the name of the plate, but they had an idea of what they were gonna order. As they both took their time to look at the menus, two men arrived through the back door, both with guns in hand, and headed to Michael and Jerry's table.

One of the men hit Jerry on the ribs with his gun. "Let's go, both of you follow us."

Michael and Jerry didn't have a clue what was going on. They didn't have a gun for protection. They had no other choice but to raise their hands and follow the men. As they hit the back part of the restaurant, Jerry looked at the red Ford and looked at Michael, as though telling him, *I told you so.*

As they both sat in the back part, one man was already in the truck waiting for them. He gave them both a bandana each with a black pillow-type bag. Jerry looked at the items they gave him.

"Are we playing cops and robbers?" he said.

The guy sitting in the back seat just looked at him. "Very funny, pinche gringo. The bandana is to cover your eyes. Then I will place this black cloth over your head.

"An all that is for?" asked Michael.

"Don't ask, just listen," said the man.

They continued to do as they were told. As the black cloth was placed over their heads, they felt the truck move. When they arrived at the location, the man told them it was OK for them to remove the rags over their heads already. They didn't have a clue where they were or what streets they had taken. All they knew was they had spent about thirty minutes on the road.

When they got off, the three men instructed them to go inside, the boss was waiting for them. Michael and Jerry just looked at each other. "We are here already. We got no other choice."

As they walked in, there was a man waiting for them at the living room. As they entered, a lady waiting for them inside took them to the living room.

"Welcome, gringos, bienvenidos a su humilde casa." (Welcome to our humble home.) "Sit down, gringos."

As Michael and Jerry took a seat, the man ordered one of the ladies to call his son. "Petra háblale al Junior ese cabron habla el gabacho mejor que yo." (Call Junior. His English is way better than mine.)

When Junior arrived, he introduced himself to Michael and Jerry. He then followed to give his father a kiss on the forehead and asked what he could do to assist him.

"Mira, Junior, voy a ocupar que me les traduscas esto que te voy a cominicar. El ahijado me hablo me pidió que por favor involucrará ah estos gringos en la venganza que nos vamos a cobrar. Párese que El Checo les debe una ah estos gringos también. Y párese ser que no se van a regresar al gabacho asta que se las cobren. Tengo entendido que son policías de la Florida y saven ah lo que le atoran. Les dices que el ataque no va ser hoy si no asta mañana. Los rivales nos van ayudar a darle el golpe fuerte. El trato fue nosotros nos vengamos y ellos se quedan con todo lo que este adentro. No me les des mucha información me los atiendes que yo ya voy de retirada."

The man got up, shook Michael's and Jerry's hands. "Amigos, me very tired. Junior will help you. Asta mañana." When he left, Junior asked them if they wanted something to drink. They both asked for a cold beer.

"Well, gentlemen, I will translate what my father just commented to me. Did any of you pick up at least half of what he said?"

"Not a word," said Jerry.

"Well, just to let you guys know, Romero is my father's godson. He has been like an older brother for me ever since. He has asked my father to help you guys out with what you guys need."

"Your father is gonna help us attack El Checo?" asked Michael.

"The answer to that is yes, but his reply was it will be on his terms, not yours. He also said it won't be done tonight but till tomorrow night. El Checo had made so many enemies in this area. My father will be getting some help from some rivals that are planning to attack as well. The deal between them and my father is we get revenge, they get the goods and money."

Michael asked, "Do you guys have a bone to pick with him as well?"

"Yes, but that ain't important right now. My father also said you guys are cops up in Florida."

"Miami actually," said Jerry. "Michael here works undercover, and I work homicide."

"So what brings you guys here? Why the attack on El Checo?"

"I killed his son in a shootout. He refused to surrender and lost the gunfight. In retaliation of that, El Checo kidnapped my ex-wife, and here we are. He has sent me several videos where he has her captive. And like I told Romero, dead or alive, I ain't leaving without her," said Michael.

"Well, glad to have you guys join us. Like my father said, we will attack, but it won't be until tomorrow. I will show you guys up to your room. My father's conversation with total strangers is limited. He is helping you guys out because of Romero. Otherwise, he wouldn't even consider helping you guys to avoid issues. I will be communicating with you guys, and I will be the one going with you guys when we attack. Till then, get some rest. We will need it."

CHAPTER 22

Hope Stephanie Is Alive

ICHAEL WASN'T ABLE TO SLEEP that night. He kept tossing and turning. All he had in his mind was Stephanie's well-being. It had been a few days since El Checo kidnapped her. Knowing how vicious and cruel men like El Checo could be, Michael was just wishing for the best. He was being realistic over the outcome. If she was dead, he hoped she didn't suffer that much. If she was alive, he wished she wasn't tortured and left crippled for life.

Seven o'clock felt like an eternity for Michael. He knew the day to rescue Stephanie had come, but he didn't have all the information. It was past 7:00 a.m. when he woke up. As he stood by the window, he noticed more than twelve vehicles driving into the big ranch. He hurried to the restroom, washed his face, and ran to Jerry's room. He turned the knob, noticed it wasn't locked, and walked in.

"Jerry, let's go. Get up, it's time."

As he walked into the room, he noticed Jerry wasn't there. Jerry had gotten up early, had his breakfast, and was helping with the preparation for tonight. They had taken out so much ammo like you wouldn't believe it.

As Michael walked out, he noticed Jerry getting some banana clip magazines ready. Michael asked him, "What are you doing?"

"Getting the clips ready for the reload once we finish a clip. It's gonna be an automatic reload, that quick. Or do you want to be doing this tonight when we have a thousand bullets flying left and right?"

"Of course not," said Michael. "Let me help."

"It's OK," said Junior. "Why don't you come over and help lubricate and clean these guns. We don't want them to jam up on us right when we need them the most."

"Looks like you all really have all this planned out."

"We have been thinking about it for a while. We were just waiting for the right moment. I sure could use the help, will tell you that much. You got family back in Florida, Michael?" asked Junior.

"I sure do, man. I still have my parents alive and my little princess. Well, she ain't little anymore, but she's all I got."

"You are aware we are going against a very powerful cartel . You might lose your life in the attack."

"If it means to see my princess happy, I don't mind. It's her mom I am saving."

"I don't have kids yet," said Junior. "But I have a clue how the feeling might be."

"Do you know what time we will attack?" asked Michael.

"As soon as the sun sets, the backup should be arriving. Then the party will start."

"How is it that your dad is getting help from El Checo's rivals?" asked Michael.

Junior just smiled. "You ask too many questions, gringo.

"Man, I want this to start, like, right now. I am anxious to know about Stephanie. I don't want her to believe I didn't make an effort to save her life."

"The story is like this, guero. Before El Checo, my father was the most powerful and respected man in all Tamaulipas. All the way from Tampico to Nuevo Laredo was his territory. He always did his business the old-fashioned way. Under the radar, never got caught until now. It's just a myth. They can't prove anything on him. When I was born, my father dreamt of passing his power to me. But my dreams were set on something else. I didn't want to live always in fear of death by the law or rival wars. So I told my dad I wanted to study, so he sent me to Harvard. After a few years, I became a lawyer. Now I help my dad, not in the way he would have loved, but I am still there. Since I didn't take my place as I was supposed to, my father stepped down in power. He gave it away to the new era. That's when El Checo came in and took control of what my father once had. On his way to power, El Checo killed one of my dad's best friends, Romero's father."

"Does Romero know this?" asked Michael.

"No, but he will after today. My father said it was time the truth came out. Why didn't your father take revenge then?"

"That would only start a turf war over something my father didn't want to pursue anymore. But he promised that one day he would avenge the murder of his best friend. Then you guys showed up having issues with El Checo. Romero asked my father for some help, and here we are, Michael. Life has made us brothers in arms."

"It sure has. Hey, Jerry, you hungry?" asked Michael.

"Nah, had breakfast with Junior this morning, but thank you anyways. Damn everybody ate already."

"It's OK, head over to the kitchen. The ladies are always preparing food. My father has so many workers. They always stop by every so often."

"Well, if it's like that, be back in a bit."

For the remainder of the day, Jerry, Junior, and Michael, along with some of the men, got everything they were gonna need for that night. As the father came out a bit past 5:00 p.m. that day, he got with Junior to try and set up some strategy attacks.

Michael and Jerry saw them from a distance but didn't want to interfere. Since Junior clearly had stated his father was a quiet man, especially to strangers, they didn't want to get on his bad side. Especially after Michael knew who he was now. They quickly finished the war preparation and gun cleaning.

Out of all the guns they had cleaned and loaded up, there were two guns Michael liked a lot, and he put them aside. He knew those would be his fighting guns. Two 9mm Berretta chrome with black handle. Jerry was happy with his AK-47. He as well had put one aside. A little after they had put aside their war toys, vehicles started to arrive one after another. Some arrived in trucks, others in dune buggies. It was close to fifty men or so that had arrived to help out; that wasn't including the men Junior and his dad had. *Let's not forget me and Michael as well.* Out of all the men that arrived, two got close to Junior and his dad. When they showed up, Junior made a sign to get closer as well. As they got there, Junior pointed out and made the other two aware: "These two gringos are with us. El Checo has his wife captive. Whoever finds her, let's try to get her out alive. Now let's be smart and safe at the same time. We don't have a clue what we are going up against. Nobody has ever infiltrated his home. We are going in with our eyes shut here, guys."

"Actually, Junior, I have," said Michael.

Everybody looked at Michael, and Junior replied, "You have? How is that?"

"It's a long story, but remember I told you I worked undercover? Well, my last case accidentally turned out to involve him. He wanted to know me, and he invited me to his place. I don't remember how to get there, but I do remember the guys mentioned something about going towards Los Alacranes area, or something like that. Once you hit the road, that takes you to his place. You have to pass about three rings of security. He has about twenty to thirty men at each one. That's only if he is there. If you find less men at each ring of security, no sense in attacking. He won't be there."

"Looks like you did your homework, gringo. That's really gonna help us out a lot."

As soon as Junior got all the information Michael had given him, he turned around and translated everything to the other men and his father. As Junior finished, his father walked over to Michael and Jerry and shook their hands.

"Junior diles a estos cabrones que gringos con las agallas que se cargan ellos son muy difícil de encontrar. Que va ser un gusto y honor para mi morir peleando al lado de ellos dos."

After his comment, Junior gave him a hug, and the father gave Junior a kiss. Junior looked at Michael and Jerry and stated, "My father said it's hard to find two white men with the courage you two have. If he dies today, it will be an honor to do so with two brave men like you guys."

That comment gave Michael and Jerry hope. They weren't the two crazy gringos from Miami anymore. He actually saw it as an honor to go out and fight with them. With that inspirational comment the father had given them, they all got in the vehicles and drove away.

From Romero's father's home to El Checo's home, all Michael had in mind were Stephanie and Casey. If by the grace of the Almighty he still found Stephanie alive, he could take her back home and Casey could still live happily ever after. If by the fortune of God she had been killed, he honestly wouldn't know what to do. What would he tell Casey? He wasn't prepared for that.

As soon as they arrived, Jerry took Michael's hand and asked him to pray together. They had stopped a few miles before they reached the first security ring. They were assigning people what to do and what areas to attack first. As they did that, four .50 caliber army trucks arrived. With them, an army truck with more than twenty-five solders as well. With them was Romero at the front line.

As he got down, he gave Junior and his father a hug. He approached Michael and Jerry and shook their hands. "I didn't want you guys to think I would allow you to come to my country and have a party without me. I have a surprise. It will arrive in fifteen minutes. It's on its way. That surprise will lead us the way. Followed by these four .50 caliber trucks. We will follow behind them. Everybody, get ready. The fun is about to start."

Michael and Jerry got back in the vehicle. They had arrived in. Michael got his two guns, a few clips in his pockets, and waited for the so-called surprise.

Out of the blue, they heard a helicopter approaching. As it got closer, it marked the start of what had been the most horrific gun battle Michael had ever been in. As they approached the first security ring, sure enough, it had about thirty men. The helicopter had killed a few. The four front trucks had killed a few more. They just kept going. Based on what Michael could see, they had instructed the last three trucks to stay behind and battle with the men that would still be alive.

Between the first and second rings, they had a space of about ten miles. As all trucks went through, they headed out to hit the second security ring. As they hit that one, these guys were a bit more alert. They were able to eliminate two of the frontline army trucks. But they still managed to drive through and kill a few of El Checo's men. As all but the last three stayed behind, they continued to drive forward. Then all of a sudden, they saw a huge ball of fire impact the ground.

At that point, they realized the third security ring had shot the helicopter down. As they drove through, El Checo's men also eliminated their remaining two .50 caliber army trucks. But they still managed to drive through. They could hear in the radio where they were ordering four trucks to stay behind on this security ring. They were also calling the last trucks that stayed behind, if all men were dead, to head to the following ring and help each other out.

Straight ahead, the moment Michael had been waiting for. Honestly, at this moment, he didn't know whether to go straight and look for El Checo and get his revenge or go straight in and look for Stephanie. What he wanted was to be there and shoot his way in, one or the other. As they arrived, it wasn't as easy as he thought. El Checo had more security than the government of the United States provides for the president.

Shooting his way through with his two Berettas wasn't easy, but he made through. Michael was glad he had a great friend. Jerry was fighting his way through right next to him. Jerry had his back, and Michael had his. The bad guys were falling like roaches fighting for their life after a spray of Raid on them. It took them about an hour or so to gain control of the yard. Little by little, they fought their way into the house. As they entered the house, it was then that Michael saw Pedro covering El Checo.

It was at that point that Michael's heartbeat accelerated. He wanted to just get up and run at them. He wanted answers, and he wanted them now. If it wasn't for Jerry, honestly, Michael could say at that moment he could have been killed. As Michael tried to run to them, Jerry got him by the shirt and pulled him back.

"You need to calm down, Michael. We've been through a lot for you to come and mess everything over a stupid decision. Don't lose their sight. Their location is our target. We came together, we leave together."

So with that in mind, they fought their way toward them. Michael knew Pedro saw them from a distance because at one point, he got up and tried doing what Tony Montana did in his movie. He stood there and shot in their direction until he ran out of bullets. It seemed he hoped he would get them with so many rounds coming their way. The rest of the men stayed behind, fighting their way while Michael and Jerry fought their way toward Pedro and El Checo.

They were winning their way toward them, and quick. It wasn't until Jerry got hit in his right leg that they slowed down a bit. As he got hit, Michael saw them turn right into a room. At that point, Michael had assumed they had them surrounded. He wanted to keep going at them so bad. But leaving Jerry behind didn't feel so great either. As Michael stood there taking cover and shooting back, covering Jerry as well, he saw Jerry remove his belt and wrap it around his leg. And then he tapped Michael on the shoulders. As Michael turned around, Jerry signaled him to keep going.

As they went into the room Michael had assumed they had gone in, they were nowhere to be found. It was as though the earth had eaten them alive. Jerry questioned Michael twice, "Are you sure they came in this room?"

Michael looked at him and replied, "I am positive they came in here and didn't come out. We need one to keep guard while the other searches. We are missing something. There's something we ain't seeing."

"What are you talking about?" asked Jerry.

As Jerry asked his question, Romero ran into the room. I knew you guys would be the ones to follow. You guys want to have all the fun without me. Romero saw Michael staring at the walls and picture frames.

"You're looking for that button or lever to take you to his hidden rooms, ain't you."

"I saw him come in, and he hasn't gone out. If this room has no way out, by all means, there's a hidden wall somewhere."

As Jerry was guarding, he replied, "So that's what you meant you guys keep looking I will keep guarding." As he made that comment, he leaned on a small table with a lamp for support. He didn't want to put all his weight on his injured leg. As he did that, he moved the table, causing him to lose his balance and almost hit the floor.

But at the same time, one of the four bookshelves moved, opening a door for them. As it opened up, there was one of them on the other side. He unloaded his gun several times on Michael and the others, making it impossible to go in. Then Romero just smiled at them and commented, "Us Mexican officers always have a plan B."

He pulled out a flash grenade and threw it in. It didn't take long after the bang for the bullets to stop. They went in right after. It turned out they had left three men guarding that walkway just in case someone had found it. That walkway led to a tunnel with two routes. One of them led to another walkway that gave them a straight shot to God know where. And the other had some turns here and there.

What caught Michael's attention was the trash can with food wrappers in it. Like they were eating or feeding someone. He looked at Jerry and Romero. "You guys take that route. My gut is telling me to take this side."

Jerry wasn't to convinced about the split-up. I am going with you," he said.

"No, Jerry, you help Romero on this one. Just make sure you guys kill all men on sight. Don't leave me any behind. If I hit a dead end, I will go back an follow you too."

"I am coming back for you," said Jerry, and then he left with Romero.

Michael slowly took the other direction as cautiously as he could. He didn't have Jerry anymore. He had to guard both ends for his own safety. He didn't want any surprises like the men behind the secret door. As he walked down a few hallways I started hearing voices at a distance. I wasn't able to make out what they were saying it was all in Spanish. Michael knew for a fact they were pissed off because of the loud noises at times. Where was Romero and his flash grenades when you needed them.

As Michael approached slowly, he couldn't make up where they were, but he knew he was close. His heart started pounding with joy when he was able to make out some of their comments. Michael heard them saying something about that pinche gringa, and he knew they were talking about Stephanie. As he approached the last corner, he saw that no one was guarding it, and that allowed him to get closer. As he did, he was able to tell there were three men. One was guarding Stephanie, and the other two were arguing or discussing the attack plans.

Michael quietly checked his ammo and realized he didn't have enough to fight them for long. He still had four bullets in his gun and one last clip put away. He saw Stephanie on the ground. If he shot at waist level, he would still miss her. He removed the near-empty clip and reloaded it with the new one. If Pedro could do his Tony Montana move, so could Michael. As he got the courage to risk his life and Stephanie's, he quickly hit the hallway and fired his gun, unloading his full fifteen-round clip on Pedro's men.

When he stopped shooting, all three men were on the floor, and Stephanie was screaming in fear. Michael confirmed all three were dead and then approached Stephanie to make sure she was OK. As he touched her, she started to kick away. She couldn't see it was him because of the way her head was covered and taped. Michael called out her name, letting her know it was all OK.

It was then when she heard his voice she calmed down and broke down in tears. There were clear signs she had been tortured, and she was obviously in pain. But the most important thing was he had found her, and she was alive. As he untied her, she quickly hugged him and asked for Casey. Michael told her she was fine back home with his parents. She questioned him about why they had done it. At that point, there was no reason to tell her the truth. She was alive; that was all that mattered.

In that same room, they had found drugs covered with some blankets and a big wooden crate. Michael had run out of ammo killing the three men, but they had left their guns behind. He got one and gave it to Stephanie. He told her he was gonna have to put her in the crate for safety. He still had Jerry and Romero to help out, but she refused. She had those blankets covering her face for so long that she didn't want to be in the dark any longer.

"I will go with you," she said.

Michael didn't like the idea, but he understood her point of view. "OK, fine, I got the front, you guard my back, understood?"

She just bowed her head and followed him out. It wasn't until they hit the hallway back to the one Jerry and Romero took that Michael felt a big sense of relief. Junior and his men had found the open shelf and had taken a walk to make sure nobody was alive.

"You're OK, Michael? How about Stephanie?"

"I am OK, she's alive, thanks to God." As Michael made his comment, Stephanie made the last turn. She got scared and was about to shoot away, but luckily, he took the gun away on time. He told Junior that Romero and Jerry had taken that walkway before he had rescued Stephanie. Junior wanted him and Stephanie to head out to the vehicles.

The home was clear. They had won the battle, but El Checo couldn't be found. Michael asked a few men to take Stephanie out and then headed out with Junior to look for Jerry and Romero. They followed the walkway. From a distance, they could hear shots being fired. As they got closer, they saw the walkway led to an exit set up with an airplane strip for easy landing and getaway. There were a few bodies on the ground where Romero and Jerry were, but not one of them was of Pedro or El Checo. When they got to the strip, Jerry just looked at me with a look on his face that said, *They got away.*

CHAPTER 23

He Took Casey

THE HOME LOOKED LIKE A world war battlefield. Dead bodies everywhere, not counting the injured ones. Romero still had his men, confirming they weren't leaving anybody alive. He felt they had done enough harm in his homeland to keep them alive. As they were regrouping with Junior and his father, Romero came to us. As he got close to us, he hugged his godfather and gave him a kiss.

"Thanks for the help. Together, we finally brought peace to this town again." He hugged and kissed Junior as well. Then he approached us. He shook Stephanie's hand. "Glad you're alive, ma'am. He shook Jerry's hand and then mine. "Glad to share that battlefield with Miami's finest. I would go to battle crime with you two by my side anytime. If you all ever have a question or need help or are here on a vacation, look me up. Would be more than happy to help you guys out."

"We did a great job, guys," said Junior. As soon as he made that comment, one of Pedro's rivals' main guys showed up. He gave his report of how many were down and how many were alive. Junior's father said he was still working on that. The man also told Junior's father what they had found and how much money was involved. Junior's father just made a hand signal to him. As they had agreed, he could have it all. He had enough pleasure running El Checo out of town.

Junior's father and that man made a pact in front of Romero. They promised to keep the peace among themselves and avoid innocent casualties. But they promised to work together again if someone else came back into their town and caused trouble.

As they said their goodbyes, Michael helped Jerry get in the truck. Romero ordered one of his men to take them to the hospital. Then after that, to take us to the bridge. When they arrived at the hospital, they didn't notice he had taken them to the military hospital. They patched him up and gave him crutches. When I headed out to pay the bill, the soldier just signaled that it was OK, it was on the house. As they got out, the soldier driving them around asked if they were gonna stay at a hotel since it was late or just go ahead and cross over to the USA.

It was a bit late, almost past midnight. They were a bit tired and hungry, so they looked at him and said, "Can you take us to a restaurant?"

He dropped them off and wanted to wait for them. They told him it wasn't necessary. They would have dinner and maybe then, just cross over or maybe get a room for the night.

As they finished eating, Michael asked Jerry how he felt. He was good; the choice was ours. Stephanie didn't think about it twice; she wanted to cross over. She didn't want to stay in Mexico any minute longer. They got a taxi and told the driver to take them to the McAllen International Airport. He said it was out of his way; the closest he could get us was somewhere in Hidalgo.

Michael didn't have a clue where that was. They weren't about to go get lost, so they just asked him to take them across the border. They would get another taxi on the other side. As they were about to cross over, text messages started to come in. Some were from Casey, others from Sally. The ones that caught his attention were the ones that came from El Checo. It was three picture messages and a regular message. One picture message showed his parents' home completely damaged. The other showed his home completely damaged. And the third one showed Jerry's home completely damaged. Those were signs he was pissed off. He sure didn't like the surprise attack they gave him.

His text message said, "Hide your family all you want I will find them." Michael showed Jerry the pictures and the message.

He just looked at Michael and said, "Mine are at my in-laws. I don't think he will get to them."

"Mine are up in the vacation home up in the cabin. If they went through personal papers, they might have found the cabin address. I might have to call the chief on this one. I might need his help. I have no other choice."

"Let me call him," said Jerry, "see what he says." When the chief answered, Jerry gave him the details, letting him know they were back and they were doing good. The chief asked to talk to Michael.

When Michael got the phone, the chief asked how he was doing. Michael replied he was OK. The chief asked about Stephanie. "A little bruised and frightened, I should say, but alive," replied Michael.

"Jerry said you were gonna need some help?" asked the chief.

"Yes," replied Michael. "I was wondering if you could spare some help, a car or two to keep an eye on my parents and my daughter just till we get back."

"Sure," said the chief. We could do that. Do you have an address?" asked the chief.

"I sure do," said Michael. It's over by Lake Placid. Here it goes."

As the chief wrote down the address, he assured Michael his family would be safe. "Let me even call this in a.s.a.p. You guys don't worry, and I want to see you guys tomorrow morning."

"We will be there," said Michael. Thanks, Chief." As they were in line to cross, Jerry and Michael had totally forgotten about the excess money they were carrying. When it was their turn, the officer doing the checkup wasn't too happy with the picture he was seeing with them. Two men, one with an injury, and a woman who had been beaten and who still had dried blood on herself. He asked all three of them to get off and followed to separate Jerry and Michael from Stephanie.

Another officer continued to search the kangaroo pouch bags they left in the taxi. When he saw the amount of money each had, he signaled to another officer.

Michael and Jerry just looked at each other. Then Michael whispered to Jerry, "The money, it's still in the waist bags. I put them in the trunk, and I totally forgot about the money. Do you have your badge with you?" asked Michael.

"Yes, it's here in my boot, how about you?"

"Same here, I didn't leave it behind. Should we jump in and tell them who we are."

"No, it's OK, let them do their job. When they ask, we tell them. I am curious what they are asking Stephanie. Do they think we hurt her and we are holding her for ransom?"

"Something like that," said Michael. "What else could it be now they found the money? I bet it doesn't look good on our end."

One of the officers that was doing the vehicle inspection got the driver and took him for questioning. The other approached Michael and Jerry. "Can both of you follow me, please."

As they entered the building, she pointed to the seat. "One of you sit there, the other follow me."

Jerry took the first office and sat down. Michael took the second an did the same. The officer approached her commanding officer and gave him the information. He looked at the paperwork and instructed her that he would take over. He approached Jerry first and questioned him about the lady with them. Jerry turned and looked at Michael, and the officer called him out on it.

"Sir, I am asking you. I need a response. No need to look at your friend." As Jerry made an attempt to grab his badge from his boot, the officer on the spot pulled out his gun and instructed Jerry not to move.

Michael saw from the glass cubicle what was happening, and ran over to Jerry. Another officer from a distance saw what was happening, and he made the call of what was going on. By the time Michael got to where Jerry was at, the cubicle was swamped with border patrol officers all with their guns out, some pointing at Michael, others at Jerry.

As Michael and Jerry turned around and realized all the officers were around them, Michael tried to explain to them that he was gonna reach for his boot but stated over and over again that he didn't have a gun.

The officer in charge told him not to move and hit the ground. Michael tried telling him he was an officer and was gonna reach for his badge. The officer again instructed him to hit the ground and extended his arms once on the floor. As Michael hit the ground, they turned around and asked Jerry to do the same. While they both were on the ground, the commanding officer instructed one to pat them both and look for that badge they were talking about.

As they were both patted down, no weapons were found, just the badge as they had claimed to have on them. The officer gave them to the commanding officer. As he examined them, he yelled out in a sarcastic tone.

"Are these legit, gentlemen or counterfeit bought back in Chinatown?"

Michael responded, "They both are legit, sir. I am an undercover agent for Miami Dade, and this gentleman by the name of Jerry Sanders is Homicide Division."

The commanding officer instructed his men to put their guns down. He asked Michael, "Who is your commanding officer?"

"Chief White. He should be able to confirm our information."

"You, sir, you wait here," he told Jerry. "And you, sir, go back to your cubicle," he told Michael.

As Michael and Jerry both went to their areas, he continued to his desk to make some calls and confirm they were who they said they were. It took about an hour or so, but when he came back, he joined them together. "Do you guys care to explain what's going on? You hit our crossing point, he is injured, and you both have a woman half beaten to death. She has told us a story, but we need to confirm your side. On top of that, you guys are carrying more than the allowed amount in cash."

Michael looked at the officer and then looked at Jerry. "It's gonna be a long story, but here it goes …" After he explained everything that had happened, he followed to show him the text messages he had received from El Checo. By then, Stephanie had already came out. Her story added up with what Michael had said. They got their stuff, and all three were released. By then, the taxi had returned to Mexico.

Michael, Jerry, and Stephanie walked over to a burger restaurant called Whataburger. They each got some coffee and got another taxi. The driver took them to McAllen Airport. When they arrived, the first flight out wasn't till 6:00 a.m. That was a few hours away. Stephanie asked Michael for some money. She headed to the souvenir shop, got some items, and headed to the restroom. When she came back, she had changed into the items she had purchased. She did look a bit different. Michael looked at her.

"If you would have done this before we crossed, it would have been a different story for all of us."

"Michael, don't start, please. I have been through a lot. I honestly don't need this from you right now."

Michael realized his comment was out of place. It just wasn't the right time for it. "I am sorry, Stephanie. I didn't mean to sound rude. I am just glad you're alive. I hope time will heal your wounds and memory. Let's look forward after this. We have a child we need to worry about."

"Easy for you to say, Michael. You weren't the one that got kidnapped and tortured. Oh my god, I forgot to call Jason. Need to let him know I am OK. I bet he is worried. We were at home having a Netflix night when all this started . They kidnapped me and held me captive."

"Who is Jason?" asked Michael.

"Please, Michael, at this stage, after being divorced for so many years, you're gonna get jealous? Jason is the guy I am dating. We are getting married next year. It ain't a scene of jealousy Stephanie. Just asking, because the day you got kidnapped, at your home in the living room was a dead man. He died of a head shot, that's the reason I am asking.

"Oh my god!" screamed Stephanie, followed by some tears. She got up and took a walk. She still couldn't believe what Michael had just told her. After she left, Jerry got close. "Maybe that part could have waited till we arrived back home."

"Now or then, what difference does it make? She needed to know. She has me for support right now. Once we arrive, my concern will be Casey and my parents."

"You know what you're doing. It was just a thought," said Jerry. After waiting a few hours, their time had come. They were calling out their flight. Michael got his phone and texted Casey and Sally to let them know he was on his way. He called his father as well. He wanted to let him know everything was OK. He also told him Chief White was gonna send some officers over to be on the lookout. They would help out if something happened before he got there.

"See you at 2:00 p.m." He hung up and joined Jerry and Stephanie to board the plane. It was a little past 2:00 p.m. by the time they hit Miami International Airport. As soon as they got off the plane, Michael turned his phone back on. He asked Stephanie if she wanted to go to her place, or where did she want to be dropped off?

She looked at Michael and asked him if it was possible she could spend time with Casey, but at his place. She did say she didn't want to go back to her place just yet. The memories of the kidnapping were too recent. Michael thought about it for a while. He could take her to his parents. He was sure they wouldn't mind. But he had Sally to think of. He did owe her that respect.

He looked at Stephanie. "Let me make a call, and I will get back to you on that request." He called Sally, and while the phone was ringing, he got some voice mails and a few text messages. But he didn't bother to look at them just now. As Sally answered, she was glad to hear his voice. She told him how worried she had been for his well-being. Michael didn't give her the full details of what had happened, but he did let her know everything had come out OK. Michael then told her why he was calling her.

After hearing Michael's news, Sally just stayed quiet and then replied, "We ain't married yet, Michael. You know what you have to do. It ain't about her, me, or you. It's about Casey. You do what's best. But thank you for letting me know. I would have felt awkward if I would have arrived at your parents' and she was there."

"Your point of view is all I needed. We just landed, let me call my parents, see Casey, and maybe tonight you can come over, or we can meet up."

"Sounds good," said Sally. "Keep me posted."

As Michael hung up, he looked at those messages he had received. When he opened the first one, just as he was looking at it, he yelled out to Jerry. Michael showed him the picture. It was a picture of Michael's parents' home. It was a total mess. El Checo's men had turned it upside down. Right below, it had a message that said. House number 1, no princess. He continued to open the next message. It was another picture message. This one was from Michael's home. They had done the same, but this time, the message said, "House number 2, no princess." When he opened the third message, Michael threw himself to the ground, knees first. He was grabbing his hair as tears were coming out and screaming at the same time.

"You will pay for this."

As Michael made those comments, Jerry took the phone away from him, and Stephanie approached him.

"What's going on, Michael? What happened to my Casey." Jerry took a look at the phone. Sure enough, it was a picture of El Checo holding Casey. She had a blindfold on, with her arms tied with gray tape. At the bottom, the message said, "Look what I found."

Stephanie asked Jerry to see the picture, but Jerry refused. He put the phone away, got a hold of Michael to control him and calm him down. As he calmed down, Jerry sat him down on one of the seats in the waiting area. After so much commotion, an officer approached them, asking if they needed some help. Jerry showed him his badge and informed the officer everything was under control.

After Michael had regained control of himself, he called his parents on the spot. The phone must have been off; it sent him to voice mail on the spot. Stephanie kept asking what was going on, she wanted to know. Michael told her the same guys that kidnapped her had Casey now. He didn't have the all the details, but he would keep her posted once he got more.

After hearing such horrific news she hugged Michael on the spot and continued to cry. Michael asked her to be strong, promised her everything would be OK. He needed to be strong to be able to do his part. In order for him to do that, she needed to be strong. He was gonna need the support. It was his little princess they were talking about. As Stephanie calmed down, they hurried to their vehicle, which they had left behind when they flew to Texas a few days ago.

As they drove away, Michael told Stephanie he didn't have a safe place other than a hotel. The people that took Casey didn't know they were in town. So any hotel would be OK for Stephanie to stay in. They chose a Motel 8 a few miles away from the airport. Michael booked her in for a whole week. He gave Stephanie some money just in case she got hungry. He instructed her not to come out that much if possible, to order whatever she wanted but preferably have it delivered to her room. He would stay in touch with her as soon as he had some information.

After they dropped her off, Michael turned his sirens on and headed to the cabins where his parents and Casey were staying. He asked Jerry to call Chief White to ask him about the situation. If El Checo had found his parents' place, were where the officers that were supposed to be guarding the place?

The hour's drive felt like an eternity for Michael. He was concerned about his parents. What was getting him more frustrated was that Chief White wasn't answering their calls. Jerry tried calling the station. They informed Jerry he wasn't in. Chief White had taken half of the day off since 11:00 a.m. When they arrived, Michael parked his vehicle way close to the entrance. There were no signs of cops in the area. There was a chance El Checo's men were still in the area. As they got off to plan out what they were gonna do, Michael realized they didn't have any guns to defend themselves with. That pissed him off more.

As he started showing his frustration, Jerry asked him to calm down. He opened the trunk of his car and showed him what he had stored up. There were enough guns and ammo to defend themselves if they had to. Michael got a 9mm gun and strapped on a 12-gauge with some ammo. Michael looked at Jerry. "Let's work the same concept. I take lead. I got the front, you guard the back."

"Sure will," replied Jerry. "Just take it easy. I can't walk that fast."

"Sounds good. Let's go," said Michael.

As they got closer through the woods, Michael signaled Jerry. Sure enough, as they had stated, there were some men waiting for them. One of them was smoking a cigarette outside the cabin. Michael signaled Jerry to head over to the side of the cabin. He knew once he shot the man, whoever was inside was gonna rush out and start shooting away. His plan was to hit the side of the cabin, shoot the man down, and, whoever was inside, hopefully, would exit the side Jerry had taken as soon as they heard shots.

As soon as Jerry was in position, he signaled to Michael that he was ready. Michael took the man down. Sure enough, as soon as Michael shot three rounds, four men came rushing out the door. To their luck, they came out and ran toward Jerry. He was able to take two down but started to take shots from the remaining two. They got too concentrated on Jerry that they didn't bother to scope out the back side.

Michael slowly moved up to the cabin and took them out as well. He signaled to Jerry to hold off, there could be more inside. As he moved in to take a look through one of the windows, he saw his parents tied up. His father looked badly injured, but no other men appeared to be inside. He signaled to Jerry that the coast was clear.

When they opened the door, his mother was making them signs, as if she was trying to say one man was still inside. There was no other place but the restroom to hide. Michael got the shotgun and pointed it toward the restroom. Before the man could even look out and surprise them, Michael walked toward the restroom unloading his shotgun . After the sixth shot, he got his handgun and continued shooting toward the restroom.

When he tried to open the door, sure enough, there was a man hiding inside. Three shots from the shotgun had ended his life. They untied his parents. His father was badly beaten and bruised. As he was being untied, he whispered to Michael, "I am sorry, son. They caught us by surprise."

"Don't worry, Papa. It will be OK. We will get Casey back. Let's take you to the hospital. That's my concern right now." After he dropped his father off at the hospital, he told his mother he would be back. He had some issues to take care of. His mother told him she understood and not to worry about them. Besides, her husband was a bit beaten up. She knew for a fact he wasn't coming out in a day.

As Michael was leaving the hospital, he called Sally to let her know what was going on. He told her he still had some things to take care of. He would be back later to see his father. Michael headed back to the cabin. Jerry asked him about it. Michael told him he didn't have a clue where they held Casey. All he had left to do was go back and see if anybody left any clues behind and take it from there.

CHAPTER 24

Looking for Casey

A S THEY LEFT THE HOSPITAL, Michael and Jerry were heading toward the cabin. They hadn't heard from Pedro or El Checo. They didn't have an idea where they could be. Michael's last hope was for them to leave some clues behind. On their way to the cabin, Michael pulled over to the side of the road. Jerry just looked at him.

"What happens now? What you got in mind?"

Michael just looked at him. "It doesn't add up, man."

"What doesn't add up?" asked Jerry.

"How the hell did El Checo find my family? Nobody knew of this summer cabin but my family."

"Didn't you say the day you spoke to Chief White if the bad guys went through your stuff they would find the address?"

"Yes, but that was for Chief White to believe. We don't keep any information on the cabin back home. All the tax and bills go straight to the PO Box we have for the cabin."

"So what are you trying to say, Michael?" asked Jerry.

"I got a feeling the chief is the second officer working for El Checo."

"Are you fuckin' kidding me, man? Are you going insane?" said Jerry.

"Jerry, just listen to me, let me explain. When Captain Ross was murdered, he didn't want the second autopsy. Throughout the whole process, he gave me an attitude. I have been waiting for some video surveillance where it showed Captain Ross taking the drugs out of the building. He came up with the sorry excuse that it got misplaced. Now the cabin. Nobody knew about it, but as soon as I give him the address, El Checo takes Casey. On top of that, he was supposed to have two officers here taking care of my parents. Where are they? Weren't there yesterday when we arrived. Now he hasn't answered you. He knows what's up. He is just buying time to come up with a great story."

Jerry just shook his head. "You're fuckin' crazy, man. I will back you up on everything, but not on the Chief White story. If he hasn't answered, he has his reasons, man. Come on, the man has a personal life. Wife might be sick. He could be sick," said Jerry.

"I am sticking to my story. It sounds more legit." Michael put the car in Drive and continued driving toward the cabin. He knew he needed to act fast. They had Casey. There was a bigger chance Casey wasn't gonna have the same luck her mom had. If Checo wanted a payback, getting to Casey would be it. He didn't have a clue where Pedro or Checo were. He was waiting for a text, a sign, something that told him where they could be. But no messages were coming in.

When they arrived at the cabin, Michael and Jerry both walked around the area. They couldn't find anything that could tell them Pedro and El Checo's location. The dead bodies didn't have any identification; they didn't have a clue who they were. Jerry asked Michael if they were gonna call in the shooting. Michael gave him a "yes, but not yet."

"Jerry, do you know anybody working at the station that can track us some text messages? I mean, like them telling you where the message came from or what area."

"I can make some calls. Why, what you got In mind?" asked Jerry.

Make your call, give them my number, let them know we need the location of every call or text that comes to my phone, please. While you do that, I am gonna take some pictures."

Michael walked around to every dead body and took some pictures. He sent them to the same number that had been sending him the pictures and videos of Stephanie. The following message was attached with the photos: "Is this all you got."

"OK, Jerry, now we wait. What did your contact say?"

"He will keep me posted. He said he was a bit busy bit will try his best."

"Sounds good. I am sure it's gonna work. If it doesn't, I don't know what else to do, Jerry."

"Be patient, man. It will work out for us."

"You can call in the bodies now, if you like," said Michael. "As soon as the cops show up, we give them our side and get out of here."

"I love your plan," said Jerry.

As they waited for the officers to arrive, Jerry finally got a call from Chief White. As the phone rang, he showed Michael the phone so he could take a look at the screen. As Jerry answered the call, Michael got a text from El Checo. Michael showed the text to Jerry, giving him a thumbs-up. When he opened it, the message said only, "That's just the beginning. Paybacks are a bitch."

As Michael finished reading the message, Jerry put his call on Speaker. The chief was questioning their actions. He had just gotten a call about some shooting and some dead bodies. And once again, Jerry's and Michael's names came up. He was requesting them to calm down a bit. There was only so much he could do to defend and protect them both. As he was lecturing Jerry, the chief's line once again was ringing. He told Jerry he was gonna place him on hold while he answered the call. When he came back, the lecture got even worse.

"What in the hell, are you two requesting numbers to be tracked? Who are you guys trying to get now?"

"We are trying to track El Checo's location, Chief."

As soon as Jerry said that, Michael hit his shoulder and gave him a sign to quiet down, not to give him all the information. As soon as the chief heard El Checo, he yelled out it was enough. He clearly said Michael needed to step back and let him get some officers to do the job. As Michael was the main witness, he was only gonna jeopardize the case. Jerry just gave him the "OK, I will let him know" and continued to hang up the call.

"Jerry, man, why did you tell him what our plans were?"

"We need to report to him, Michael, regardless of your crazy idea."

"I just hope we didn't get your friend in trouble."

"I don't think so," said Jerry. As soon as he made that comment, Jerry got a text with an address. It also said "not exactly but within a 25-mile radius. My boss caught me, that's all I could get. Can't help you out anymore for today, he's keeping an eye on me."

Jerry replied with a "thank you owe you one." As soon as Jerry showed Michael the address, he wanted to leave on the spot.

"Michael, hold on, we need to wait for the officers that are supposed to show up."

"Jerry, understand, if we wait, he is gonna get away. I know what I am telling you."

"Michael, just calm down. He don't have anywhere to go, just be patient. We have an address already, that's a start." Michael was so close to leaving Jerry to make the police report while he went out and took a look at the address they had given them. But he and Jerry had been through a lot. He couldn't do that to him. He had no other choice but to wait till the officers arrived.

When they arrived, Michael let Jerry do the talking. Jerry explained to the officers what had happened he did let them know he tried searching them but found no identification on them. As soon as the whole report had been given, Jerry gave Michael a sign, letting him know they were good to go.

The address Jerry's contact had given them would easily make it about an hour's drive for them. At the speed Michael was driving and with the sirens on, he cut down the drive time by about fifteen minutes. Jerry's contact did state the address given was within a twenty-five-mile radius. The address took them to a neighborhood area. That made it a bit more complicated to identify the home they were using. Jerry asked Michael if the area looked familiar when he was undercover.

Michael replied with a negative. The few homes they used were not in that area. Michael told Jerry since they knew he was a cop, he had a feeling they must have changed stash houses by now.

"What are we looking for?" asked Jerry.

"Well, to start, we are looking for homes that have SUVs parked outside. Next, we need to look out for guards outside the home. If El Checo is around, he likes to have lots of security taking care of him.

Once we identify those two items, we should find the home. If we have to go street by street, home by home, we will do that."

They had already driven by two streets. By the time they were about to hit the third one, Jerry noticed a black SUV leaving a home on the other end of the street. As soon as he saw the vehicle, he pointed it out to Michael. Michael went ahead and drove in the pickup truck's direction. As they passed the house that the vehicle had left. It didn't show any movement, no sign of any more guards. It was as though they had already moved out.

Michael continued to follow the vehicle to get a closer look at the passengers. As he was about to catch up to them, the driver of the SUV hit the gas pedal. Michael knew on the spot that they were hiding something. As he tried to catch up, he turned his sirens on to do a traffic stop. He wanted to know why they had sped up. But the men had no intention of slowing down. They had no option but to call for backup.

When the backup showed up within no time, they had the truck surrounded. Once the truck came to a complete stop, four men from the truck tried to flee the scene. Jerry was in no condition to run, so Michael took one guy. One of the backup officers was from the K9 unit, so he took one guy, and he released the dog on another one. The other backup had two officers. They took the fourth guy.

Within minutes, all four men were handcuffed and brought back to the truck. All four of the men were sat down next to the truck. Michael asked them all why they tried to run away from the police. He gave them an opportunity for them to let him know what was in the truck before they took a look. All four of them tilted their head down; no one wanted to speak.

Michael gave them a second chance. "Look, gentlemen, if I search your truck, if I find guns, drugs, or money, you're looking at federal time, not county time. I will make sure you get federal time for this. Now is your chance."

One made an attempt to speak out, but another man kicked him to stay quiet.

"OK, you had your chance." Michael gave the police officers the signal to search the truck. One officer requested Michael to take a look at what they had found. Michael looked at the men being arrested and said, "Excuse me, gentlemen, I will be back. Do not, I repeat do not, go anywhere."

The four men had no way of going anywhere. They had handcuffs on and plenty of cops around them. They looked at each other with a face like, was he trying to be funny? When Michael got to the truck, to his surprise, it had ten kilos of cocaine and five suitcases full of cash. It sure looked like more than 2 million dollars with that cash. They also found four AK-47s, two on the driver's side and two in the back seats.

Michael looked at Jerry. "That's the house they are using. We need to go back. Maybe my Casey is still there." Jerry requested them to arrest the men and log the drugs and money.

Michael pointed out the man that wanted to speak up. "I need that man separated from the rest. We will run an errand. When we are done, we will personally interrogate all four men ourselves."

"What are you trying to do?" asked Jerry.

"You didn't see the man? He looked like he was gonna speak up. But the guy with the black shirt kicked him, like he was trying to say 'Shut up.' If we get him alone, and if we arrest El Checo, he can be a material witness against him. We have enough to arrest Pedro, but we have nothing on El Checo."

"I see what you're saying. That could help us in the long run. Let's go, we have that house to go to," said Jerry.

When they arrived, the home looked empty; there was nobody in sight. They both got off a few houses away from it. They walked up to it slowly. One went in the front door, the other went in the back. It didn't take them long, but they both met up inside. Sure enough, the house was empty. It had signs they were there. They searched the basement. Same thing. There were also signs they were feeding someone there.

Michael looked at Jerry. "We were close, Jerry. If we came straight to this address when we got it, we could have found them at that point. But no, someone wanted to wait," said Michael.

"Man, I ain't gonna argue with you. I know how much it hurts knowing they have Casey. But you also know we have a job to do. I am understanding your pain, now understand my point of view."

"OK, Jerry, I ain't gonna argue with you right now. Let's head back. That man is our only lead to finding them. If they had those drugs and money, they were probably the last ones to relocate to a new location. Someone told them we were coming."

Here we go again. You're gonna say Chief White. Didn't you say they said at one point they had two officers on their payroll? We found out about one. Maybe that other one is letting them know. It doesn't mean it's Chief White. Get that out of your head," said Jerry. "We got one sooner than later. We will get the other one."

"OK, sounds good," said Michael. "Let's head over to the station."

When they arrived to the station, he got a message from El Checo. The message said, "What did you think I have him now."

Michael was so pissed off he wanted to get a location he needed to get Casey as soon as possible. He got to the interrogation area and asked where they held the gentleman he had requested to be separated from the rest. When he walked in, he rushed to him as though he wanted to shake the life out of him.

"Tell me where you guys took my Casey!" Michael yelled at him several times. The guy was lucky Jerry was right behind Michael. He had to interfere and asked Michael to step out for a bit. As Michael got control of himself, he realized what he had done. He went ahead and told Jerry to take over; he was gonna go get something to drink.

When Michael came back, Jerry had already calmed the guy down. He was cooperating a bit more with them. As the guy was about to tell them what they wanted to hear, someone banged on the window. Jerry and Michael stepped out of the room. Chief White was waiting for them.

"I hope you guys did everything by the book. That gentleman's lawyer just stepped in and doesn't want us to interrogate his clients any longer."

As Chief White was giving them the information, Michael got a text. It read, "I want my money back and I want it back right now. Or you won't see your daughter alive."

"Is there a problem?" the chief asked Michael.

"Yes, sir, there is." Michael showed the chief the message.

The chief stayed quiet. "Damn, Michael, that's gonna be a tough one. Give me an hour. Let me see what I can do for you."

"Thank you, Chief," said Michael.

Jerry looked at Michael. After the chief left, Jerry made a comment. "Do you still think he is on their payroll?"

"I don't know, Jerry. We don't have the money yet. Besides, you trust everybody. You shouldn't be like that, Jerry. One day life will force you to clearly open your eyes and see life the way it really is. But from now till then, let's be patient on the matter, my friend."

"What will happen if Chief White can't help us with the money?" asked Jerry.

"Don't say that. Not even joking around," replied Michael. "I have no other option. I don't have that kind of money. If it were to happen, I will have to do what Captain Ross did on his case."

"Go in and steal it, you mean?" said Jerry. "Are you crazy? I ain't helping you on that one," he replied.

"Don't worry, my friend. I wouldn't ask you to jeopardize your job." As they kept talking about the money, Jerry got a call from the chief. A two-minute call, and then Jerry hung up.

Michael looked at Jerry. "So what did he say?"

"I told you, Michael, that man is on our side. He was able to get the money for us."

Michael looked up to the sky. "Thank you, Jesus." He texted El Checo: "You will get your money with one condition I get my daughter back first."

A few minutes later, he got a reply. "You ain't in no Conditions to give me terms Michael."

Michael replied, "Okay, your loss just like you lost your power in Mexico all your drugs here in the US . Now you're about to lose what's left of your fortune. This is all you have left to make a comeback, and you know it. My terms or you don't get jack."

Jerry looked at him. "It's Casey's life you're playing with. Are you sure you want to go ahead with this?"

"Jerry, I have a 10 percent chance I am getting her back. That's the reason I am giving him a hard time now. If I lose Casey, he sure ain't getting this money back. Not without a fight, that's for sure."

"Another fight? Are you serious? We don't have Romero and his men, Junior, and his father. Michael, open your eyes for a minute. Let's be realistic."

"Jerry, you be realistic. He is on our turf, why can't you see that? This battle is won without a fight."

"But knowing him, he ain't going down without one."

As he made those comments, he got another text from El Checo: "Meet me by the warehouses by the Port. There you will get instructions of where to pick up your daughter."

CHAPTER 25

Going After El Checo

MICHAEL AND JERRY HEADED OUT to their car. Michael had a plan, but he wasn't too sure it would work out. He knew for a fact that he was outnumbered. He and Jerry didn't stand a chance against El Checo.

"So what's the plan?" asked Jerry.

"That's what I am thinking right now," said Michael. "We can't go with full force and try to get Casey. He will see us a mile away. If so, he will either kill Casey or take her somewhere else. That will only make it worse, or harder to get her. Now we need to keep in mind he still has one man on his payroll telling him our every move."

"That only makes it more difficult for us to give him a surprise attack," said Jerry.

"Yes, sir, but we do have options," replied Michael. "Let's go, I have an idea."

"Yes, sir, you lead, I follow," said Jerry. Both got in the vehicle and drove away. On their way to Miami, Michael called his father right quick to see how they were doing. Michael didn't give him too much information, just the basic. Told him he was a bit busy at the moment. He was just calling to see how they were doing. He would call him later.

Once he hung up, he called Stephanie as well. He wanted to know how she was doing. She was a bit frightened still. She was doing as instructed by Michael. She wasn't coming out from her hotel and just ordering food by delivery. She asked about Casey. Michael changed the conversation on her, told her he was a bit busy but would call her back in a few minutes. He wanted to call Sally as well, but with Jerry in the car, he would prefer a more private conversation with her. So he just went ahead and sent her a brief message.

As he texted away, Jerry asked him, "You didn't answer my question, Michael. So what's the plan?"

Michael looked at him. "You ain't gonna like it one bit, but here it goes. Pedro has some enemies here in Miami. I saved his ass from them once. They are our option."

"Option. Are you crazy?" said Jerry. "Two officers will go down to their turf, ask for help, and expect to come out alive? Damn, Michael, I honestly don't know if every day you get smarter or just plain crazy."

"Jerry, look at me, that's our only option if we want a surprise attack. Or do you have another plan or the manpower to hit them good?"

"Well, if you put it that way, that's the reason I said you get smarter every day."

"Very funny, crippled man," said Michael. "Let's just hope they still want some revenge on Pedro, and we shall be OK, trust me."

"*Trust*, hmm, you still think I don't trust you after everything we have been through?" said Jerry.

"Not at all, man. I am very deeply indebted to you. I don't know how I will repay you for everything you have done. Since day one, you haven't left my side."

"Yeah, and don't forget this bullet I took as well," said Jerry.

"Yes, Jerry, the shot as well," replied Michael. "God has been on our side all the way. I don't think he will leave us now. We won't lose a thing if we try."

"If your plan works out, great. If not, well, we can't say we didn't try. When they arrived at the bad neighborhood, four men were out at the entrance of the complex. You couldn't really tell if they were armed or not. Michael got his gun and left it in the car and proceeded to get out of the car. Jerry, still buckled up, just looked at Michael. Well, Jerry, are you coming or you gonna stay and take care of the car?"

"Without a gun, you better believe I am gonna stay and take care of the car."

"OK, be back in bit. If you hear shots, leave the area and call it in." As soon as Michael took a few steps away from the car, he yelled at Michael, *wait* . . . I can't let you go alone. We are in this together. Let me go with you."

"As they approached the four guys, Michael showed them their badge. The men tried to run; one was about to pull out his gun on them. Then Michael showed them he wasn't armed. We didn't come here to take you guys down. We are two off-duty cops, and we have an offer for your boss. If he likes the idea, we can negotiate. If not, we can simply just turn around and leave."

"What's your offer?" asked the man.

"Tell your boss I can give him Pedro's location. He knows what Pedro I am talking about."

"Wait here," the guy said. "Let me see if the boss is available for you guys."

It took him about fifteen to twenty minutes by the time he came back. "The boss wants to see you guys, but we need to search you guys first."

"Sure, no problem," said Michael.

After both had been searched, they were escorted into the building. They went up to the third floor into a room. As they walked in, a man requested for all men to exit the room. He kept only his best man by his side.

"So my men tell me you two are off-duty officers and you have some information on Pedro. How true is that?" he asked.

Michael introduced himself, and so did Jerry. Michael took the lead and continued to explain the situation to the man. Halfway through the conversation, the man interrupted Michael. Long story short, you want us to hang your dirty laundry, is that what it is?"

"Not completely," said Michael. "We can take him down. He will be arrested and serve his time. Well, that's if we don't kill him when we attempt to arrest him. Knowing him, he won't go down easy. But that's our plan. We found out by the great vine you guys and Pedro have a pending issue. If I ain't mistaken, you haven't found him yet to get your revenge. Well, we are offering you that opportunity. We will give you about one hour to do your part, then we go in and do our part. You don't have to if you don't want to. Keep in mind once we get him, he ain't coming out."

"How do you know about that pending revenge we have with him?"

"Honestly, I was working an undercover case. He came in here to charge his quota. I clearly don't know what took place in here. But he did some damage. It came out in the news, if I ain't mistaken. He took some of your men out, and you guys just took one of his."

"That is correct," said the man. "He actually killed my older brother."

"Well, the offer is available," said Michael. "We can't stay long. We are gonna hit him tonight or tomorrow morning. If we don't hear from you, we go in as planned. If you decide to get your payback, like we said, we will let you know what time we will get the arrest warrant so you can know what time to go in. After that, we will give you an hour. If you're still there within that hour, you will force us to take you down as well.

"You two got some courage coming to my territory and making me a great offer. How did you all know I wouldn't kill you too? You ain't armed. We can very easily do so."

"You're smarter than that," said Michael. "You want your power back. That's something Pedro took away from you besides your family member. If we take him down for you, yes, you will get your power back, but not the respect. If you go out and do it yourself, you will gain both power and the respect you once had. Last call, man. We are leaving already."

As both Michael and Jerry got up and headed toward the door, he made a sign to his right-hand man not to let them go. What guarantee do I have you won't do the same to me when you take down Pedro?"

"There ain't none," said Michael. "I am a cop, you're a dealer. We are bound to meet one day. As long as you don't bring up the heat upon yourself and stay off our radar, you're good to work. Keep in mind, this is just a courtesy visit. Once we leave, we weren't here and we have never met."

"Sounds good," said the man. "What time are you guys going in?"

"We hit at 10:00 p.m. You have from now till nine thirty to make your move. Make sure you're out by nine thirty, just in case we arrive early, you guys ain't around."

"OK, thanks for the heads-up. If you guys ever need anything, a favor, you name it. I will be here. Saul Sauceda, better known as El Zauz."

"Thank you," said Jerry and Michael.

"We will keep you in mind."

"Wish we could say the same, but our jobs would be on the line if we do. Hope you understand," said Michael. After they made their last comment, they both got escorted out and went their way. Michael was waiting for the chief to give them a call to let them know where they were gonna meet up to get the money. He knew the time had arrived, and he was anxious. He wanted to go get his Casey back—he just didn't have the manpower to do so.

Jerry looked at Michael. "That was a great idea, Michael. Have El Zauz and his men going first, then we hit them."

"Hope El Zauz and his men win the battle. With this hurt leg, I ain't much of a help. But one thing is for sure. I ain't gonna back away now. I will be there for you till the end, my man."

Time was running out. Michael didn't have the time to wait for Chief White. They both went over to meet up with an old friend of Michael's. With their last confrontation with Pedro and his men, they were down on ammo. If they were gonna be short on manpower, they had to make sure they had the extra ammo. The time had arrived. It was about to be 9:00 p.m. He had a fifteen-minute drive to the place they had instructed him to go.

They took their time, didn't want to arrive, and they both would still be in the middle of the gunfight . Michael hadn't gotten any more text messages, so it meant the meeting point hadn't changed. They were still meeting at the same place they had agreed on. It was the same place El Zauz and his men were gonna be as well. When they arrived, the area was clear, with lots of bodies on the ground and blood everywhere. Someone must have called in the shooting. The radio was going crazy, and you could hear the sirens from a distance.

"Let's go," said Michael. They needed to walk down the area and make sure they didn't leave any evidence linking them to Pedro's rivals. As they both walked down the area, not one body was alive. They were still warm, but all dead.

Michael had Jerry looked for evidence, and he would look to see if any of them was Pedro. Jerry was able to confiscate a laptop that had two bullet holes and took it to their vehicle. Michael didn't find Pedro but did find a man that looked a lot like Yanko. He noticed Jerry walking out with something in his hands, and he threw it in the trunk. As he walked up to him, a few cops arrived at the scene.

Jerry and Michael quickly displayed their badges and allowed them to do their work. They both gave their information to the lead investigator, and right after, they were informed they could leave if they had to. As they got in the vehicle, Michael quickly texted El Checo, questioning him of his findings. He got a message a few minutes after. The answer was he was told to turn the computer on and enter the password given.

Michael informed them the laptop had been damaged in what appeared to be a shootout at the address they had given him. As they drove away, he got another message with an address. He showed it to Jerry.

"What do you think?" asked Michael.

"I don't know. You got any more aces up your sleeve?" said Jerry.

Michael just smiled. "I wish I had a whole army to get them all and get my Casey back. Check your phone, Jerry. It's funny the chief hasn't called about the money."

"Nope, no missed calls on my end," replied Jerry.

"On this next visit, it's just me and you," replied Michael.

"Yeah, I know. I'd say that's more than enough to getting the job done," replied Jerry. "Let's go get them."

Michael drove to the next address they had given him. He knew he didn't have a backup crew to help out. When they arrived, they parked a few blocks away . As they got off, Michael took the radio with him as they slowly approached the area. They could see a few men guarding the area. Michael was pissed off this sucker was playing them.

"He ain't even here."

"Not enough men to protect him, you mean," said Jerry.

"Yeah, he normally surrounds himself with a lot of men. His plan is to come out and have one of his men take us out.

"What you gonna do?" asked Jerry.

"Let's play his game." Michael got his gun out, asked Jerry if he was ready, and walked toward the building. As they got closer, they both started shooting, eliminating men as they got closer. As they got cover, they started getting shot left and right. Michael got the radio, and called it in. He gave a description of the situation, gave them the address, and put the radio away. He gave Jerry a sign, and he got up and started shooting, giving Michael a chance to move to his next spot.

As Michael moved, he did the same for Jerry till they arrived at the door. Michael heard a voice saying, "Come on, pinche guero, the boss said you would show up. Let's go, cabron, show yourself."

The voice didn't sound too familiar, but if on the last shootout Yanko was dead, he assumed this one could be El Pilas, like always send someone else to finish your job. Michael made some signs to Jerry to change guns. They were gonna shoot their way in and hit the nearest hideout for cover. As they both got their AK-47, they both shot away, Pilas and his men had no option but to take cover, giving Michael and Jerry time to run to their next cover spot. Now the gunfight was inside the building. Michael and Jerry were wining this fight.

A few minutes later, Michael heard on the radio that some cops had arrived. He responded with, "Front side is under control. Take the back side."

Michael lowered the radio and gave Jerry a thumbs-up. "They are here," Michael said.

As they both fought their way in through the front, their backup was already fighting their way through the back door. It wasn't long after all men had been killed. Not one wanted to give up. They all fought till their death. Jerry and Michael looked around for some evidence to their next location. It was obvious Casey wasn't there. Jerry looked at Michael.

"They assumed we would be dead after this attack."

"They sure did," Jerry replied. "Michael, they even send their best men to do the job."

They both got their gear and once again went over to the officer in charge, gave them their story, and went their way. Jerry drove this time. Michael had to text El Checo with the surprise they were both still alive.

He got a message right quick. "I see you too scum bags are still alive. Go to this address I want your daughter to see her father die in my arms then I will finish her myself like you did with my boy."

Michael knew this was their last stop. There was no going back. Jerry noticed his face change. He grabbed his partner's shoulder. "Don't you worry. We will come out alive on this one as well. We have before, and we will this time as well."

"Thanks, Jerry. I am sure we will. Just glad to have a friend like you. What do you have planned for our next address?"

"I honestly don't know. I am sure I will come up with something." As he was thinking, he decided to call his father. He had some fear they both wouldn't come out alive. He didn't have a plan B. It was just him and Jerry against all of Checo's army. When his father answered the phone, they spoke about their day, and his father asked him for an update on Casey's situation.

Michael gave him the address of where they were supposed to meet up with El Checo. When his father asked what the plan was. Michael stayed silent.

"We don't have one, Pops. We have used all our resources. This time it's just me and Jerry against all of them."

"You two are really crazy. How long will it take you to get there?"
About an hour or so," said Michael.

"Don't do a thing until I call you back, you hear me?"

"What you mean, Pops? I need to get Casey."

"We will, Michael. This time we will do it my way. Wait for my call. Don't do a thing till I call you."

It wasn't till another thirty minutes later. By the time they arrived at the address given, Michael and Jerry got their full gear on, with extra ammo. They knew very well they weren't gonna have the time to be coming back and forth for ammo and guns. Michael was getting anxious. It had been thirty minutes since they had arrived, but they couldn't do a thing since he had orders from this father not to move till he got his call.

As he waited, the phone rang. It was his father.

"What took you so long?" asked Michael.

"Be patient. I wanted to make sure it was good to go before I gave you a call. It's all set. Make sure you stay on clear areas, especially windows. If you want the extra help, are you ready?" asked his father.

"Of course we are," said Michael.

"The party has started, and good luck." After he said that, he dropped the call.

"What was that about?" asked Jerry.

"I don't have a clue. He just said to stay out in the open, mainly visual, and to stay close to the windows at all times. Whatever that meant, but OK."

As they both walked their way through some trees toward the main fence, Michael noticed from a distance the extra security. "Looks like this is the place we had been looking for."

"The man is in the house," said Jerry.

As they both closely approached the home, the guards inside started shooting away, defending their post. But not one bullet was being shot at Michael or Jerry just yet.

Jerry looked at Michael. "What's all that commotion about? We haven't even shot one round. Is that your plan B?" asked Jerry.

"Man, I told you I was out of options. This time it was gonna be just you and me," replied Michael. "That I don't have a clue what all that is all about."

As Michael and Jerry watched, men on high grounds were falling like flies. "If we are gonna attack as well, now is the time," said Jerry.

"I was waiting for you to say that," replied Michael.

By the time they hit the gates, the manpower guarding it was at four men. The rest were dead on the ground. As they both approached and fought their way in, they too noticed all the dead men on the floor. They both looked up and thanked the Lord for the help. Whoever it was wasn't showing their face but was doing one hell of a great job about it.

On all sides of the home, men were going down. Not even Michael and Jerry had an idea what was going on, but they were marching forward faster than what they had expected. The home they had arrived to was a two-story ranch-style home that took up five acres. It had more windows than the Sears Tower in Chicago. Jerry looked at Michael. "We are about to hit the home. Are we gonna have the same help inside as we are having outside?"

At that point, Michael thought about what his father had said. He looked at Jerry and replied, "As long as we stay on clear areas, especially windows, we should be good."

"What the hell are you talking about?" asked Jerry.

"I don't have a clue, but those were the last words my father said before he hung up on me. So far it has been going great, so how about we do as he said?" replied Michael.

As they approached the home, Michael could see Pedro from a distance. He was trying to take cover behind a thick wooden pillar. Next to him was who appeared to be El Checo. They both were receiving those mysterious bullets as well.

As Michael and Jerry approached the main door, Michael signaled to Jerry: same scenario as before, change weapons and shoot their way in for cover. As they made their way in, Pedro and Checo called him out.

"It had to be you, pinche guero, but guess who's gonna pay for it?" As he made that last comment, Michael saw El Checo run one direction and Pedro the other.

Michael signaled Jerry to take Pedro, and he would take El Checo. Michael followed him into a master bedroom with a double-sized patio glass window. By the time, he walked in, El Checo had Casey in a chokehold, pointing a gun to her head.

"You take another step, and I blow her brains out," said El Checo.

Michael put his arms up in the air. "No, come on, let's work this out. You said you were gonna get me first. How about we take care of this with a fistfight. Winner blows the other's head off."

"Don't shoot. I am putting my gun down."

As he did, he taunted El Checo. "Come on, show me what you got."

Checo just laughed and threw Casey to the floor. "I am sure gonna enjoy this."

Before he put his gun away, he shot Michael, causing him to hit the ground. As Michael slowly got up from a shot to the arm, El Checo now taunted Michael.

"Now let's fight."

El Checo had an advantage, but Michael was defending himself pretty good. A few minutes after the fight had started, Jerry walked in on them. Michael instructed him not to get involved. Jerry informed Michael he had shot Pedro. Nobody in the house was alive. As he gave him that information, he put his gun away and let El Checo and Michael keep fighting without getting involved.

As Michael was beating the life out of El Checo, Chief White showed up with a bag full of money.

"Well, it's about time you showed up, Chief. Michael's got this. I don't think we need the money anymore."

As he made those comments, Michael turned around, looked at Chief White, then at Jerry. Michael yelled out, "It's a setup. He's the second officer on their payroll."

By the time he said that, it was a bit too late. Chief White had already shot Jerry twice in the chest. That caused Jerry to hit the ground fast. After shooting Jerry, he pointed his gun at Michael.

"You get off that man and walk straight to me." Michael saw the big window in the room. He knew that if he stayed in clear view of that window, he would have a chance of coming out alive. He disobeyed the chief's order and walked over to the window.

As he had his hands up, he questioned the chief about his actions. The chief ignored him and just commented, "You couldn't listen, could you. I told you many times over and over, stay away. Let us take care of it, but no. He had to be the good cop. Look where it has brought you now."

As he made those comments, the chief had walked into the clear view of the window. Without realizing his future and life as an officer was about to end. He kept on nagging to Michael of his actions.

Soon after that, El Checo was just getting up, ordering Chief White not to kill him. He wanted to have the pleasure of killing the officer that killed his boy. By then, Jerry was still conscious but couldn't move much. He had a bulletproof vest on, so the bullets had bruised him, just causing pain. At that moment, Michael lowered one of his hands, pointing at Chief White. He made a gun signal with his fingers. A few minutes later, a shot was heard. Chief White died on the spot from a bullet wound to the head, dropping down to the floor.

As he hit the ground, his gun did as well. At that point, Michael and Checo fought for the gun, and the fight started all over again. This time Jerry was good to get up. He got his gun out and walked toward Michael and Checo. As Checo was about to reach for the gun to shoot Michael, Jerry put the gun to his temple.

"You touch it and you die."

Michael got up and walked toward Checo and kicked him in the face, knocking him unconscious. He then walked toward Casey, who this whole time had been screaming and crying. As he got close to her, he told her everything was OK. He removed her blindfold and untied her arms. As soon as she was released, she hugged Michael so tight.

"I wanna leave, Dad. I don't want to be here any longer."

"We will, baby. Just need to make some reports. Then we will be gone for good."

As he was picking up Casey from the floor, six snipers dressed in black were walking up the stairs.

Jerry and Michael covered Casey and pointed their guns at the men coming up.

"It's OK, men, we are on the same side. Who do you think had your back all this time?"

"It was you guys?" asked Michael.

"Yes, sir. Let your father know mission was successful. If he ever needs us again, he knows where and how to find us."

All six of them turned around and left the scene.

CHAPTER 26

Family Cookout

ICHAEL WAS GATHERING WOOD WHILE his Pops was cleaning the barbecue pit. His Ma was with Casey in the kitchen, seasoning the meat and getting some side dishes ready for the big cookout. Casey stood by the door, staring at her father and wondering what he was doing. When Michael noticed Casey's long stare, she told him, "I love you" in sign language.

Michael replied, moving his lips, "Me too." As he said that, she opened the door and ran toward him and gave him a hug, followed by a kiss.

"Dad, is Mom coming over to the cookout?" asked Casey.

"She sure is. I have already sent Jerry to go get her."

"Who else is coming over?"

"Well, Jerry and his whole family are coming over. He will do me the favor of bringing your mom with them. Then we also have Sally coming over with her kids."

"You're gonna have Mom and Sally together, are you serious?"

"Now, baby, we have all gone through a lot, so don't worry over a small problem like that. I have spoken to Sally, and she is OK with it. I didn't tell your mom anything about it. So it could be a surprise to her when she arrives and see Sally here. I will introduce her as the future Mrs. Brown, you know."

"If it's that serious, Father, well, if you're happy and she is happy, why can't I be as well?"

Jerry and his family, together with Stephanie, were the first to arrive. As Stephanie got off the vehicle, Casey ran to her and received her with a big hug. They both started to cry. Stephanie calmed her down and told her everything was OK.

As Michael got closer to hug them as well, Sally arrived with her kids. As Casey and Stephanie were feeling a bit better, both walked with Michael to receive Sally and her kids. As Sally got off, Michael introduced Stephanie to her. Michael had Casey show the kids around while the food was being prepared. Sally and Stephanie walked over to Ma and Jerry's wife and sat together, all of them chatting away.

Jerry, Pops, and Michael were by the barbecue pit . "You're doing all right?" asked Jerry.

"Yes, sir, couldn't be better, man."

Mr. Brown said, "Jerry, that plan B you pulled out yesterday was one hell of a plan."

"Thanks to you, sir, we are all here gathered today. I owe you my life. Oh, come on, you have done more for Michael. Let's call it even and enjoy a great time."

"We sure can, sir," said Jerry.

Michael said, "Jerry, how in the hell did you know the second officer was, in fact, Chief White?"

"I had a gut feeling all along. He kept giving the runaround, especially with reinvestigating Captain Ross's case. Up to now, I haven't received the video of the day the captain stole the drugs. I got a feeling if it wasn't him, it sure was Officer Ramirez that also came out on that video that's the reason he didn't want me to see it. He kept on telling me to stay away from the case. It was in his best interest it stayed as a suicide and accidental murder. Now the day of the shootout with Pedro and Checo. I waited and waited for his call about the money. I never spoke to him, so he didn't have Checo's address. When he arrived with the money, that confirmed he was the second officer we were missing."

"I am glad you were wearing your vest. Otherwise, you wouldn't have been here."

"He sure did give me two solid hits to the chest," said Jerry. "So what are your plans?" asked Jerry.

"Well for now, spend some time off, enjoy this lovely family time. Maybe next year, I don't know how you feel, but I honestly think me and you made an excellent dynamic duo. Batman and Robin didn't have jack on us. So what you say, Jerry, do you have room in your patrol car for a partner?"

"Man, you know I would love to have you work with me. Have you told the family about it?"

"No, I was waiting for Sally and for you guys to arrive. Now that my whole family is complete, I can give them the great news. I won't be doing undercover work anymore. Me and you will be the best in the Homicide Division Miami has to offer."

As for Checo, his day in court came. He got life in prison for the drugs and double kidnapping and for murder.

CPSIA information can be obtained
at www.ICGtesting.com
Printed in the USA
BVHW061934200822
645087BV00001B/113